A PROMISE OF DAWN

A STORY OF ADVERSITY, INSPIRATION, AND THE EVERLASTING POWER OF HOPE

CHIKAODI E. CHINWUBA

Divine Works Publishing LLC., Royal Palm Beach, Florida U.S.A

© 2023 Chikaodi E. Chinwuba

A PROMISE OF DAWN

All rights reserved. No part of this publication may be reproduced, stored in a retrieval system, or transmitted in any form or by any means, digital, electronic, mechanical, photocopying, recording or otherwise without the prior permission of the publisher or in accordance with the provisions of the Copyright, Designs, and Patents Act 1988 or under the terms of any license permitting limited copying issued by the Copyright Licensing Agency.

The views expressed in this work are solely those of the author and do not necessarily reflect the views of the publisher, the publisher hereby disclaims any responsibility for them.

ISBN-13: 978-1-949105-54-4 (paperback)
ISBN-13: 978-1-949105-61-2 (hardback)
ISBN-13: 978-1-949105-55-1 (eBook)

First Edition Published: 10/11/2023

For Information or Bulk Orders Contact:
Divine Works Publishing
Royal Palm Beach, Florida USA
561-990-BOOK (2665)

DIVINE WORKS PUBLISHING
INSPIRE. INFORM. TRANSFORM

www.DivineWorksPublishing.com

DEDICATION

*In dedication to the loving memory of my father,
S. O. Chinwuba,
who passed away before publishing his physics books.*

TABLE OF CONTENTS

Acknowledgments — vii
Introduction — ix

Chapter 1 Two Wrongs Don't Make a Right — 1
Chapter 2 Family Always First — 7
Chapter 3 The Adventure — 17
Chapter 4 When Tragedy Strikes — 25
Chapter 5 Fear and Harassment — 33
Chapter 6 Lured by Lies — 41
Chapter 7 Unfolding of a Lifetime Opportunity — 51
Chapter 8 Beauty and Brains — 63
Chapter 9 Success Makes a Merry Heart — 75
Chapter 10 The Reward of Resolve — 83
Chapter 11 The Nuances of Naivety — 95
Chapter 12 Choosing for Life — 101
Chapter 13 An Unexpected Turnaround — 111
Chapter 14 Building a Lasting Foundation — 123
Chapter 15 Two Hearts Beating as One — 135

About the Author — 145

ACKNOWLEDGMENTS

To my mother for her unconditional love and perseverance in ensuring her children received quality education despite the odds.

To my husband, for his undying love and care.

To my siblings for their continuous support.

I thank the Almighty God who is the giver of life for providing, directing, and guiding me while writing this novel and for making it a reality.

INTRODUCTION

A Promise of Dawn provides insights into the adventurous and challenging life of a promising child, Elly John, who weathered the storms of life, like most great men and women do, rose to be a shining star, and was widely recognized for the positive impact she made in the lives of both individuals and couples through her seminars and counseling sessions.

Elly, the first daughter and third child of her parents, was a source of renewed hope for her mother, Beatrice, who despite all efforts to feel loved and accepted by her husband's family felt rejected, unloved, and unwelcomed. Elly's grandmother wanted her dad to marry a woman of her choice. Yet, despite the cold treatment from her in-laws, Beatrice maintained a kind and positive disposition towards them all, particularly her mother-in-law, and hoped that someday things would improve.

Although things didn't turn out as she hoped for, she was consoled by the fact that her husband loved her deeply and assured her that his feelings for her would never change despite how negative the attitudes from his family members remained. He was known to be a man of his word and he kept true, loving her faithfully up until his last breath.

Elly was the epitome of joy and happiness to her parents, and she was greatly loved by them, especially her father, with whom she shared a special bond. Her life's journey was off to a smooth and graceful start—due particularly to her father's attentiveness and love. He was reliable and always ready to help her when needed. Subsequently, and due mainly to the early demise of her father, she struggled throughout her teenage and early adulthood years. She and her siblings received limited help from family members after their father's death thus, they learned to be independent at a young age.

Despite her grief, their mother, Beatrice who had limited source of income at the time of his death, determined that all her children would attain the highest level of education possible. She honored how important this was to her late husband. She knew this would not be an easy under-taking given that their children were still quite young, but she was determined to fulfill her late husband's dying wish—no matter what it took.

Elly encountered a good deal of struggles both financially and emotionally after the death of her father and often wondered why she had to endure all these difficulties. Little did she know that those very same struggles and pains were shaping her for a great destiny and bright future ahead. Her early journey in life was riddled with numerous instances of sexual harassment, rejection, emotional and financial hardships. There were times when she contemplated giving up. However, she persevered through all these formidable obstacles and emerged as a distinguished counselor.

As her life's purpose became clearer, she came to value the difficulties she faced during her darkest moments. Realizing that those hardships prepared her for this bright future, transforming her into a source of inspiration for those encountering various challenges in life, especially in the realm of relationships and marriage. She helps them understand the importance of always maintaining a positive mindset, especially when faced with life difficulties. "Be aware that there's purpose in the pain and remember that there's always a silver lining at the end of the tunnel."

Although this book describes the adventurous life of a gifted child, which is fictional, it also aims to encourage people to understand that "life has a lot of struggles," and no one should assume that "life is a bed of roses." Our struggles often shape us for the future and should be regarded as "the stepping stones needed to attain the required heights in life."

If only we could glimpse the endpoint of our journey, we would truly grasp the vast significance and value of the battles we wage and the challenges we encounter. Remember to always foster a hopeful spirit and never underestimate the power of hope. Embrace the firm belief that a brighter tomorrow awaits us.

1 | TWO WRONGS DON'T MAKE A RIGHT

Elly was born into a family of five children, comprising three boys and two girls. She was the third child, but the first daughter of her parents. Her mother, Beatrice suffered several miscarriages after the birth of her second son and was greatly unloved by her mother-in-law, (since she wasn't the preferred woman for her son). Her mother-in-law introduced him to a lady from her town, who was also the daughter of her closest friend, for Elvis to marry, but he turned the request down, explaining that he was in love with Beatrice and no other woman could take her place in his heart. His mother employed various means to ensure her request was honored and he marry the woman of her choice, but all efforts were futile, as he maintained his stance to marry Beatrice—the woman he considered to be his one and only true love.

Due to her son's refusal and insistence towards marrying Beatrice, she decided to make life difficult for her and assured Elvis that she would never accept Beatrice into the family or consider her a daughter. Elvis paid no attention to what his mother said regarding his chosen bride since he was the one that would ultimately live with her; hence his decision would supersede every other person's view on the matter. Also, he didn't want to put himself in a situation whereby he married a woman against his will just to please his mother, while his heart was with another woman. "This is a recipe for disaster," he said.

His mother's disapproval, conveyed through her words and actions, revealed the obstacles that lay ahead if he chose to marry Beatrice. Yet, he resolved deep within himself to shield his wife from his mother and anyone else who dared to meddle in their union. Elvis paid no heed to his mother's objections because he discerned no valid grounds for opposing his decision. It seemed that his mother sought to exert control over his life by dictating his choice of a spouse. But he had grown beyond such manipulation, and thus he stood firm in his resolve.

The wedding took place despite his mother's disapproval, and Elvis was thrilled to marry the woman he loved. The marriage was blessed immediately with two boys, and then there seemed to be a delay with having more children. Elvis and his wife always wanted to have a big family of at least four children, as children were considered more valuable than wealth in those days. Most households had an average of five or six children. The delay in childbirth after their second son made Beatrice a bit uncomfortable since her husband's family placed pressure on them to have more children.

Due to the obvious aversion Beatrice's mother-in-law held towards her, she pestered her son to marry another wife claiming his wife was unable to bear more children after almost three and half years of birthing their second son. Her disdain for Beatrice was so much that at some point she accused her of killing and sacrificing the children in her womb, referencing the several miscarriages she had after the birth of their second son. Yet, despite all the negativity, Elvis disregarded his family's opinions and reassured his wife that they would have more children in due time. He made it clear that he would never marry another woman, no matter what. Elvis was known to be a man of honor who always kept his word. He was also very kind-hearted, extending helping hands to friends and family members as needed.

Elvis was born into a polygamous family, with his mother being the last of five wives which was a norm in the olden days, where men were known to marry numerous wives. Due to the polygamous nature of his upbringing, he lacked the deep connection between a child and his father, and made up his mind from a youthful age to marry only one wife, shower his family with love and attention, and create a lasting bond with his children.

Elvis's father, who was amongst the top three richest men in his town, popularly referred to as Okosisi (meaning the "great tree") died when he was about 10 years old. This meant that although he was born with a silver spoon in his mouth, so to speak, he grew up in penury, as his half-brothers (who were much older than him and since he was the first child of the last wife), took their father's properties and shared it amongst themselves. The penniless situation Elvis found himself in made him independent at an early age. He obtained several odd jobs in order to fend for himself, his mother, and his siblings.

Despite the penniless state he found himself in after the death of his father, Elvis was determined to make it through life, and he succeeded. He rose to respectable ranks, even attaining the professor title in the university where he lectured at a very young age. He also supported his younger siblings through school, with each attaining a higher level of education as desired. He was well respected for the perseverance and kindness he showered his family and all the people around him with.

Following numerous miscarriages, Beatrice was bestowed with a baby girl, five years after the birth of their second son. Enduring a precarious pregnancy, on the verge of losing the baby, fate intervened, allowing her to carry the child to term. This redemption silenced the naysayers who had cast shadows of doubt before the birth of their third child. The cruelty of those who questioned a woman's worth after giving birth to two sons astounded her. Yet, she remained grateful for the arrival of her long-awaited third child... A daughter at last.

The birth of her daughter proved a miracle to Beatrice, sparking a glimmer of hope that her mother-in-law might soften, showing some semblance of care. Nevertheless, her attitude remained unchanged, as expected by Beatrice, aware of the underlying reason for the woman's disdain. Despite Beatrice's efforts to involve her in the nurturing of the newborn, Elvis's mother demonstrated no affection or enthusiasm towards the news of her granddaughter's arrival. After the loss of her own mother several months prior to the birth, Beatrice was left with no recourse but to turn to her unfeeling mother-in-law for support in caring for the new addition to their family.

Despite enduring the harsh treatment from her husband's kin, particularly his relentless mother, Beatrice steadfastly returned their animosity with love and respect. She clung to the hope that one day their hearts would soften towards her. Alas, that day never arrived. Grasping the reality of her in-law's unyielding indifference, Beatrice embraced the decision to focus her energy on her immediate family. Her steadfast husband, defying all odds, loved and defended her, serving as her rock. That love, that unwavering support, proved enough to sustain her. She exhausted every measure to win acceptance from her husband's kin, only to bear witness to the fruitlessness of her endeavors, as they ceaselessly sought avenues to make her feel unwelcome.

Elvis observed how his wife often faced challenges in gaining acceptance from his family and empathized with her, knowing how difficult it must be to experience rejection. He advised her incessantly to stop putting so much effort into trying to win his family over and focus on other things. He assured her that his family's disapproval of her would never change how he felt, nor would it ever affect his love for her. He loved her deeply. He had chosen her as his wife and nothing anyone said or did would change that. He vowed to remain loyal to his wife. In adulthood, Elvis was known as a "one-woman guy," and everyone knew that once his mind was made up for something or someone, nothing could change that.

He had initially threatened his mother and siblings with cutting them off from his life if they continued to show disrespect towards his wife, but Beatrice pleaded with him to reconsider his stance, believing that would likely make matters worse. She also did not care to be the reason for any source of contention with his family. She could accept their lack of love for her but could not be happy knowing that she was the reason for any grudges he had with his family, especially with his mother. She also wanted her children to have a healthy relationship, as much as was possible, with their father's family and that might not happen if Elvis cut off his family from his life.

Elvis listened to her plea and decided not to go through with his intentions, since he loved her very much. Also, he remembered how stubborn his mother could be, and had he gone through with his decision to cut them off, to see if their attitude towards his wife would change for the better, it would likely not yield a positive outcome. Concluding how, two wrongs don't make a right....

2 | FAMILY ALWAYS FIRST

The entrance of the baby girl into the family filled them with immense joy and bliss. Her enchanting beauty, with her curly locks and radiant smiles captivated the hearts of all who laid eyes upon her. She became the apple of her father's eye, and Elvis was willing to go to any lengths for his precious daughter. He even took a few days off from work to support his family, as Beatrice was still recovering from the emergency C-section she underwent due to complications during childbirth. In order to ensure a swift and complete healing process, she was advised to extend her stay in the hospital for further observation, followed by additional bed rest upon discharge.

During the birth of their first son, the doctors requested to perform a C-section on Beatrice (given the circumstances surrounding the childbirth at the time), but Elvis's mother who waited in the delivery ward somehow convinced him that normal delivery was best and that it would also save him a good amount of money. Beatrice's mother was out of town for an official assignment when she went into labor, hence her mother-in-law opted to accompany them to the hospital, given that it was their first childbirth experience. Elvis relied on his mother's advice, but later realized that it was one of his greatest mistakes ever, as his wife lost too much blood during the birthing process and almost died. Thankfully, the skilled obstetrics doctors remedied the situation, saving both mother and child. Elvis vowed never to listen to his mother's advice regarding matters relating to his family. Little wonder when the doctors advised that a c-section should be carried out for the delivery of their daughter, he didn't hesitate before giving consent for the procedure to be performed.

After the birth of their first daughter, Elvis's mother was only willing to do the basic things for Beatrice to enable her to recover quickly, thus he became more involved since she needed all the help she could get at that point. Elvis considered family a top priority, he never put anything before his family and he made that clear to everyone, including his colleagues at work. Although this caused issues at certain times with some of his superiors, he maintained his stance that family came first.

He frequently revisited how he felt when he was a child, always desiring love and closeness from his father, but lacked this since their father was always busy chasing money or giving more attention to his older half-brothers and sisters. He grew up seeing parents of his close friends attend most of the school games, award ceremonies, and spend quality time with them, especially during the weekends and long holidays. They always shared the fun times they had with their parents, and he silently wished for what they had. Few times during such conversations he had stepped away from them to cry silently, as he earnestly tried to get close to his father but was not successful.

Okosisi, as he was fondly called by people around him, was mostly unavailable for his family because he was always working or exhausted from the day's work and needed to rest once he arrived home. He was an industrious and very wealthy man, but he failed to maintain and balance the home front, as his wives always fought with each other despite living in different houses within his small estate. He had very limited time to spare for his large family. As a result, the wives and children often fought for his attention, thereby leading to quarrels and fights amongst themselves. As a child, Elvis often wondered why a man would bring such troubles to himself by having a lot of wives and then having to settle quarrels continuously amongst the women.

Because of his childhood experience, he made a promise to himself: to keep a strong foundation at home by marrying just one wife and ensuring that his children would never experience the same pain he did as a child. He vowed that no matter what, work would never interfere with his family. "They could never dismiss him from work" he always said to himself, because he was making a huge impact in the continuous expansion of the university where he worked. In his view, it would be their loss if they asked him to resign. If not because of how loyal Elvis was to the university and he wanted to assist in changing and expanding its landscape within the country, he would have resigned a long time ago, as he got job offers from other universities for a more senior position which he turned down. His notable success in the expansion and growth of the department where he acted as the Head resulted in the widespread recognition of the university, hence he was sought after by various institutions. The students who graduated from his department always stood out in their workplaces due to the in-depth training and knowledge they received from his lectures, and with time, employers in the field started prioritizing graduates from the department over other candidates.

After Beatrice gave birth to their first daughter, Elvis faced a busy period at work. However, he had no choice but to take some time off to care for his growing family. He also knew that someone had to supervise their older children's nanny, as the boys were known to play in a rough manner most times, and whoever was responsible for them had to exercise a great deal of patience in order to handle these excesses. The boys went through three different nannies in one year, as they either had to quit the nanny roles due to the demanding nature of the children or they were asked to leave by their parents due to consistent harsh treatment towards the children.

Elvis and his wife wished and hoped that their next child would be a girl. Given how playful the boys were they felt a girl in the mix would make things a bit calmer. However, they also worried that the playful nature of the boys might rub off wrongly on a girl or that she could accidentally be injured while playing with them.

As a child, Elvis had a close female friend who unfortunately lost an eye while playing with one of her younger brothers. At the time, she was just ten years old and the only daughter among her siblings, consisting of about four brothers.

On this fateful day, the parents left to visit some friends, and she was playing stone catch with her second brother in the garden as the nanny cleaned up the house. As they continued to play this dangerous game, the brother threw a stone towards her, and since she was unable to catch it, the stone hit her left eye. She screamed in pain as blood gushed out.

The nanny rushed out to the garden and found her on the floor screaming with blood in her eyes. Frightened she called for help. One of the neighbors who heard the scream for help, rushed out of the house and seeing what happened, immediately drove the girl to the hospital, while the nanny called the parents to inform them of the tragedy. Upon examination, the doctor noticed that the eye was completely damaged, and nothing could be done to restore vision in the affected eye. As a result, this girl born with both eyes intact lost one of her visions due to carelessness and a dangerous play with her sibling. The parents were devastated for a while when they heard the news, but there was nothing they could do to reverse the situation.

Beatrice made a speedy recovery, surpassing expectations. The doctors consequently discharged her earlier than originally anticipated. She was advised to prioritize rest and avoid engaging in strenuous activities. Elvis and his wife eventually returned home upon being discharged from the hospital and as they pulled up, their boys ran out to greet them. They hugged their mother tightly and were overjoyed to see her, since they hadn't seen mom since she left for the hospital. As they hugged their mother, they saw their father carrying a baby, and then they ran to him, asking to hold her for a while. Elvis made sure they sat down on the parlor sofa before placing the baby in the arms of his first son. They both looked at her with so much love in their eyes and gently stroked her hair.

The boys, joyous with the arrival of their new sister, persistently wanted to touch and carry her, and often stroked her hair, which was quite soft and full of bouncy curls. All their attention over the following days shifted towards their new-born sister and Elvis noticed that they were always careful whenever they played around her, to avoid any injuries. Just like their parents, the boys loved their sister very much, and Elvis was over-joyed with how gentle they were with her. Seeing this, his earlier fears disappeared, and he knew for certain that his baby girl would always be protected by them, especially since men tend to have an instinct for protection.

The naming ceremony of the baby girl was fast approaching, and preparations were made by Elvis and his family towards making the occasion a success. Naming ceremony is usually a small event organized by the parents of a new-born to announce the child's name chosen by the parents and in some cases the grandparents to a few invited guests, which usually comprises immediate and extended families of the couple and some close friends. This event often happens on the seventh day after the child's birth, with a bigger ceremony occurring three months afterwards when the child is taken to church and dedicated to God, being the source of all creation.

Prior to the date of the naming ceremony, Elvis and his wife had chosen a few special names which they felt correlated with circumstances surrounding their child's birth and the joy they felt having her in their lives, which they planned to announce to the attendees, in accordance with tradition.

On the day of the naming ceremony, a few close friends and family members were in attendance, and they exchanged pleasantries amongst themselves. They looked at the beautiful baby girl with so much admiration and seemed to be astonished at her beauty, since she had a natural glow with very curly hair which was not very common in babies born in that part of the country.

As the ceremony commenced and it was time to call out the child's names, the second brother, who was about six years old at the time seemed to have other plans for her name. He repeatedly shouted the name "Elly" indicating that was his own chosen name for his sister. His parents wondered where he heard the name, and why he kept screaming the name even after he was asked repeatedly to keep quiet.

Since he refused to keep quiet and repetitively mentioned the name, Elvis and his wife felt moved in their spirit to name her based on the brother's wishes, and her first name became Elly. They however included other names they had written as her middle and other names, including a native name "Nneoma" meaning "Good Mother," which was chosen by Beatrice to commemorate the passing of her mother a few months before the birth of her daughter.

Elly was loved by her father being his first daughter, and especially since there's known to be a special bond that exists between a father and his daughters, particularly the first daughter. They had also waited and diligently prayed for a baby girl and God had answered their prayers, so she was a dream come true for her parents.

Although Elvis was a disciplinarian, he seemed to have a soft spot when it came to Elly, and he struggled to reprimand her when she misbehaved. Even if he refused everyone else's requests, he found it difficult to resist Elly's, and Beatrice used that to her advantage, regularly. Elly became her "go to person" when she needed something from Elvis which he might have refused otherwise.

She was deeply cherished by her father, who seldom reprimanded her, even in situations where her missteps were evident. Beatrice cautioned her husband on several occasions regarding his obvious preferential treatment, asking why he scolded her siblings, but when it came to his favorite daughter, all he did was give her a look of disapproval. "This is not enough and acceptable" she blurts out most times, explaining that this preferential treatment might make her irresponsible in the future. "There are negative consequences of not reprimanding a child when she exhibits such negative attributes" she explained to Elvis often. Well, it seemed like all his wife's words fell on deaf ears, as he paid no attention to her regarding the matter. He couldn't help himself when it came to his beautiful daughter, and he also didn't seem to understand why that was the case.

On a certain occasion, to everyone's surprise, especially Beatrice, Elly was scolded and spanked by her father for being playful during school lessons. Some might wonder how Elly, the apple of her father's eye, provoked him to such an extent. Well, it happened that she was enrolled in an after-school lesson where she decided to play more than pay attention. The teacher cautioned her continually and often punished her, hoping that she would desist from playing and disturbing the entire class. Since she failed to listen to the teacher after all the punishments and caution, he decided to report the matter to Elvis, whom he shared a friendly relationship with. They had both attended the same high school when they were younger and maintained a somewhat cordial relationship afterwards. Elvis was three levels higher than him back in college.

Elvis, as an academic who valued education, became upset upon hearing about his daughter's disruptive behavior in class. In order to address this issue, he decided to have a serious conversation with her and provide necessary discipline, (however, it is important to note that he did not use any excessive physical force).

Elly locked herself up in her bedroom and sobbed loudly because she couldn't believe that her father would scold and even spank her. She stayed in the room and bawled, refusing to leave the room till Elvis came knocking on the door and consoled her. He explained to her what she did wrong and why he had to scold and spank her for such behavior. He explained to Elly that he loved her very much, but she needed to understand the benefits of having a great education. "There are many opportunities that will abound in the future if you do well in your studies," he said. He made a lot of valuable points as he spoke with his daughter and gave her examples of the many things she could achieve in life with a good education. Slowly, Elly stopped crying and listened to her father attentively, who was seated beside her with his hands across her shoulders and speaking gently to her.

After Elvis ended his speech, she felt better and stopped crying. She rose, wiped the tears off her face, and joined the rest of the family for dinner and afterwards played with her siblings. Although she didn't realize it at the time, the wise words spoken by her father that day were going to be very useful to her in the future when he would no longer be there to help her navigate life.

A few days after this incident, the examination results of the class were published, and she emerged top of the class. This achievement was truly remarkable, both for her and Elvis. Despite her playful nature, she consistently scored high in all subjects, even among a class filled with highly intelligent individuals. This only served to highlight her exceptional brilliance, and Elvis always took great pride in her academic accomplishments and accolades. Elly's intelligence shone through as she garnered numerous awards throughout her early school years.

Although the playful nature of her elder brothers seemed to have rubbed off on her a bit, Elvis was consoled by the fact that she was brilliant, and her studies were not negatively affected by her playful nature.

3 | THE ADVENTURE

Her childhood was an exciting time filled with adventures. Like most children, she had her fair share of dangerous experiences. One such incident occurred when she was just three years old. Due to the negligence of their nanny, she found herself in a perilous situation, narrowly escaping being crushed by a passing car.

She was on her way to church with her elder brothers and immediate younger sister, accompanied by their nanny, when suddenly, the nanny who was carrying her younger sister and holding one of the brothers seemed to forget that Elly was with them. They proceeded to cross the road leaving her behind and when Elly realized that they had crossed to the other side of the road after being distracted, innocently decided to cross the road to meet her family. She didn't realize that she needed to look left and right before crossing the road. She walked gently across the road, and when she was in the middle of the dual road, an incoming car began to honk incessantly, and that was when the nanny looked back, realizing what had happened, ran back, and picked her up. "Oh my! I wonder what could have happened if the driver was speeding." Thankfully he was driving slowly and was very observant. Of course, the driver scolded the nanny for such negligence.

The incident was never mentioned to Elly's father or mother, as the nanny pleaded with the children to never say a word about it to their parents. She knew that if either of the parents heard about the incident, particularly Elvis, she would be fired for putting their child's life in danger. She even went as far as bribing them with some biscuits and jellies, and they all promised not to mention the incident to their parents.

Another occasion when Elly caused panic for her parents was when she was about nine years old. Her class teacher had planned a trip for the students to attend a children's day event out of town, which occurs yearly and had in attendance students from other schools. The event, which was held in a different city from the school, was a good way for the students to meet children from other schools and compete in sports, drama, debate, and the likes. Prior to the date of the event, parents were asked to consent to their children partaking in the event by completing the necessary documents and providing their wards with an agreed amount to cover the cost of hiring a bus for the trip. A few expenses such as feeding were to be covered by the event host.

On that fateful day, Elly joined her classmates to the event, and as the event was about to end, she mischievously agreed with a few classmates not to join the bus back home, but rather spend the money given to them by their parents to buy confectioneries as they walked back home. As the event ended, they hid from the teacher and other classmates, who eventually had to leave them behind as they couldn't seem to find them. The teacher assumed their parents might have picked them up from the event venue, since some parents attended the event and picked their wards afterwards, thus not all students were expected to join the bus back home. However, this assumption was incorrect, as she was solely responsible for the students' being they were placed under her care. One would have expected her to confirm the status of all students before proceeding to leave the venue, but she decided to take the easy way out and neglected her role as a guardian.

As the teacher left the venue with the other students, Elly and her peers came out of their hiding spot and proceeded to walk back home, all the while spending the money given to them by their parents to buy biscuits, drinks, and other sweet items. They failed to realize that it was going to be a long walk home especially for Elly whose house was the farthest among them. They didn't seem to feel the impact of the long walk back home as they chatted, laughed, and played as they journeyed back home, with each person dropping off on getting to their respective homes.

Eventually, Elly was left with only one person from her class since their houses were a bit farther and they lived not too far from each other. Suddenly the weather changed, and it began to rain, and they playfully ran under the rain while it got darker as it was approaching nightfall.

Meanwhile, Elvis and his wife were beginning to get worried that their daughter was not back home, and it was almost nightfall. They were also unable to reach either the class teacher or headteacher to confirm the whereabouts of their daughter. Since they couldn't get in touch with anyone from the school and it was getting late, they decided to leave their other children at home in care of the older siblings since the nanny had left for the day. They got into the car and drove amidst the heavy rainfall in search of their daughter, all the while praying silently that she was safe.

Luckily for the couple, they hadn't driven too far from home when they saw her running in the rain with one of her classmates. They screamed her name, parked by the roadside, and picked her up alongside her classmate, both drenched from running under the rain. They dropped off her classmate in his house and proceeded to go home. Elly sat quietly at the back of the car seat as they drove home, all the while shifting her gaze between her mother and father, since deep down she realized that she would likely be in trouble because of her actions.

As she waited to know what her parents would say or what punishment she would receive, she was surprised to see that neither her father nor mother said a word to her all through the ride home. She didn't realize that they were just happy that she was safe but were not going to express this feeling in order not to encourage such bad behavior in the future. Immediately they got home, Beatrice made a very hot tea for her daughter, wrapped her, and tucked her in for the night.

The next day, after they knew she was okay, Elvis and his wife called her into their bedroom to inquire more about what happened the previous day and why she was not in the company of their class teacher and other students. After she narrated the entire story to them, they were silent for a while as they were short of words wondering what could have happened to her on the way home. At the same time, they were overjoyed that she was safe.

Elvis eventually took up the issue with the headteacher and expressed his disappointment over the conduct of the class teacher who transported the students to the event. "It is her responsibility to ensure that children left in her custody return to their parents safely," he angrily explained. The headteacher apologized for the conduct of the class teacher and assured they would handle the matter appropriately.

In general, Elly experienced a memorable and beautiful childhood. She had much fun with her siblings and was raised in a loving home. Beatrice, who was a schoolteacher and frequently had spare time, invested time and resources in helping her children expand in skill sets such as computer knowledge. There's increasing awareness and a shift to technology, so this is a skill that will be very useful to them in the future. Due to this early exposure, Elly began to familiarize herself with the knowledge and use of computers at a young age and developed a fondness for computers, as she was always excited whenever her mother asked her to assist with typing certain documents. At first, she was quite slow with typing, and had trouble locating the letters on the keyboard. However, she never got discouraged and kept at it every day, and with time she improved.

She had lots of adventures with her siblings also, especially her immediate elder brother, Tommy, who was the most stubborn of all the children, and frequently landed both himself and others in trouble with their parents. On a fateful occasion, he landed himself and almost Elly in trouble when he took their father's car keys to spin it around, without having any prior lessons on how to ride a car. The only knowledge he had about riding cars was from watching their father ride them while in the car and he felt that it was easy. He decided to take their father's car out for a spin, with the intention of returning it before he found out that it was gone. As he plotted in his mind on how to go about it, he challenged one of his friends to a car race using their parents' cars on one of the weekends and convinced Elly to join them for the race.

The night before the fateful day which he agreed with his friend for the race, Tommy snuck into his parents room and took the car keys, with an intention to race his friend early in the morning and return the key before either of his parents got out of bed.

Elvis and his wife had a tradition of spending one day during the weekend at home as much as possible to create room for their children, hence they often got out of bed late every Saturday. Tommy, knowing his parents' pattern, decided that would be the best day to carry out his plan. He had intended to finalize the race and return the car and keys to the right positions without anyone finding out. He proceeded to the open field where he agreed to meet up with his friend, with Elly seated in front of the car. He had convinced her that the car race was going to be fun, and she agreed to join them.

The car race began, and everything seemed to be going well, initially, and they were having so much fun till their luck ran out and Tommy mistakenly drove the car into a small open drainage. The drainage was partly covered, so he missed it. Thankfully, they both came out of the car unhurt, and a few people who were present in the area helped them push the car out of the drainage. However, the car suffered a few dents because of this incident. As he looked at the dent in the car, he knew that he was going to be in a lot of trouble because their father had recently spent money to fix the car and repaint it to make it look a bit new.

He hurriedly drove the car back home and asked Elly not to ever mention the incident to anyone and instructed her to sneak back into the bedroom and act like she was still sleeping, because he wanted to save her from the consequences of his action. He immediately proceeded to return the car keys, hurriedly snuck out of the house, and went to his friend's place to hide out. He informed only Elly of his plans and asked her not to mention it to anyone. He intended to stay there for a while till their father's anger subsided after he became aware of what happened.

Elvis awoke a few hours later and abruptly decided to step outside and head toward his parked car for some unknown reason. He immediately noticed the dent and was certain that it had not been there the day before. He summoned all his children. Each one denied knowing anything about the dent or how it had occurred. He noticed that Tommy was not present, and given his mischievous acts in the past, he could only assume that he was aware or responsible for what happened. Also, Tommy had persuaded him a few days prior to teach him how to drive a car, but he had turned him down, explaining that he was too young for such lessons.

Elvis was furious regarding the matter since he had just spent a reasonable amount of money to fix and spray the entire car, and due to his son's carelessness, he was about to spend additional money to get it fixed again. He had no other option than to let the matter rest and wait for his son to get back home.

Tommy eventually returned home two days after the incident, when he felt that his father's anger must have subsided or that he was perhaps no longer angry with him, but Elvis was determined this time around to punish his son severely since he had a habit of damaging his properties and going against his instructions.

He thought up the best punishment for his son and decided that he would be expected to wash his car daily for the next few months and banned him from visiting any of his friends, especially the one he had raced with. For Tommy, that seemed like a fair punishment given the damage he had caused to his father's car. However, his sister, who accompanied him to the car race, was spared from any of the punishments. No one mentioned her involvement to their father.

4 | WHEN TRAGEDY STRIKES

Elly enjoyed a multitude of exciting experiences during her early childhood years. These etched unforgettable moments in her heart, particularly with her father. Sadly, when she reached the age of 13 and entered high school, her father unexpectedly fell severely ill and required frequent hospitalizations. Numerous doctors conducted tests in an attempt to unravel the root cause of his illness, resulting in differing diagnoses from each practitioner.

Beatrice, who harbored a distaste for driving, had no other option but to gather her courage and bravely transport him from one hospital to another, even if it meant traveling to distant medical facilities based on recommendations from relatives and close friends. She was often perplexed by the contrasting diagnoses and treatments prescribed by each doctor, yet her husband showed no signs of improvement.

Luckily, after several months of relentless treatment, there was a glimmer of hope and he was able to return home. However, mere weeks later, tragedy struck again as he relapsed. Another series of treatments commenced, but this time his care was restricted to one of the premier government hospitals, under the watchful eye of a specialist who had overseen his case during his previous discharge. Unfortunately, it seemed that he wouldn't overcome this setback as he succumbed to his illness a few days after being admitted.

Oh, how Beatrice wept upon losing the love of her life, exhausting every possible means to rescue him from death's icy clutches. Beatrice was cherished by her husband to such an extent that only death had the power to separate them. He provided her with nearly everything, and some might even argue that he pampered her excessively. Well, I suppose that's how every woman desires to be cherished by her spouse. There's a saying that goes, *"submission comes easily for most women once treated right by their husbands. A contented woman fosters a joyous home."* In Elvis's household, this sentiment rang true, as the affectionate atmosphere cultivated through their relationship was palpable even to outsiders, and the love permeated through their five beautiful children.

People came from far and wide to console Beatrice, especially her siblings, but she was inconsolable as she cried for days and ate very little. She remembered her children often and wondered how she would raise them alone, especially financially. She eventually pulled herself together and decided to face this challenge head-on, realizing that crying wasn't going to solve the matter at hand. The void had been created and nothing could fill it, but she had to keep moving. Three of her children were away at boarding schools, as school was still in session, as such they were not aware of their father's death. She thought of how they would receive the news, particularly Elly who shared a special bond and a deeper connection with her father than the other children.

She eventually summoned courage and left for her children's

school, together with her younger sister, to inform them of the sad news. Upon arrival at the school, she briefed the school principal of what happened and her intentions to take the children home for some time. The principal, who felt pity for her on hearing the sad news, obliged the request but advised her to bring them back once she could, since school exams were fast approaching.

Elly and her siblings were excited upon seeing their mother and hugged her affectionately, although they didn't understand why they had to return home amidst a school term, and why mom was accompanied by their aunt instead of their father. Beatrice asked them to pack a few things as they would be going home for a short while and assured them of returning to school in a few days. They did as their mother instructed, organized and locked up their belongings, and bid their friends farewell, explaining they would return in a few days. They couldn't explain to their friends why they had to leave school in the middle of the school term because they simply didn't have the answer.

The ride back home was exceptionally quiet, as if the children already knew about the passing of their father. Elly eventually broke the silence and inquired of her dad recalling the last time she saw him, he was quite ill. Beatrice glanced at her sister but didn't say a word and continued driving. It was at this point that Elly suspected that something bad might have happened, but she decided to keep quiet just like her siblings while their mother drove all the way home.

Upon arriving home, Beatrice noticed that their eldest son was home. He was already in his first year in the university, and Beatrice had sent word for him to come home. She hugged her son whom she hadn't seen in the past few months and asked him to sit alongside the other children in the dining area, while she dished the food. Beatrice brought out food which she had specially prepared for her children but still didn't say a word, even when they asked their mother why she had called all of them out of school. The children, except Elly, became excited at the sight of the food since they never ate such delicacies while attending school and immediately began to eat the food. Elly remained silent and kept looking around to see if her father would join them, with her gaze shifting towards her mother intermittently. It seemed like she was trying to read her mother's mind and figure out what she wasn't telling them.

    Beatrice avoided her daughter's gaze, while trying to hold back the tears already forming in her eyes. When she could no longer hold back the tears, she burst out crying, while her sister tried to comfort her and then she had no choice but to blurt out that "their father had died." As the words left her mouth, the boys sat still for a while, with tears flowing down their cheeks, while Elly stood up and walked away into the bedroom, shutting the door behind her. Her mother's sister went after her and knocked intensely, but no response was received. She decided to give her some time, while hoping she wouldn't attempt to harm herself, since it was obvious to everyone the kind of connection she shared with her father.

    For days, Elly crawled up on her bed and thought about all the good times with her father and wondered how she was going to make it through life without him. Her life seemed to be falling apart, as her most favorite person on earth was gone forever. She cried uncontrollably for days, asking God to have pity on her and return her father. She refused to either interact with anyone in the family or eat anything and turned pale as the days went by. All her mother's pleas to eat fell on deaf ears, as she lacked appetite for food. About a week afterwards, Elly was hospitalized as she had slumped in the family home due to the lack of food and nonstop crying. Beatrice was overwhelmed with fear for her child's life, causing her to weep and pray relentlessly day and night, pleading for God to revive her daughter. The mere thought of losing her was unbearable for Beatrice, as it would surely shatter her entire world. Thankfully, after three agonizing days of unconsciousness, Elly eventually recovered. Beatrice's heart leaped with joy, and she was overcome with gratitude that her daughter had been spared from the same fate.

Gradually, Elly began recovering emotionally and when her mother felt she was strong enough, she brought her back to boarding school to join her siblings who returned earlier to continue their schooling, as exams were fast approaching. Beatrice was convinced that being surrounded by her friends and siblings at school would accelerate the healing process, and fortunately, her belief proved to be true. She frequently contacted the school through her guardian to inquire about how she was faring and was glad to hear that there was a lot of improvement in her mood. She had cheered up and was interacting well at school and getting involved in various school activities.

The date for the funeral ceremony was fixed around the time schools were closed and the children were on vacation, including when the eldest brother, Tony, was back from the university. Beatrice wanted all her children to be present as they laid their father to rest. Tributes were written by certain members of the family, including Tony and Beatrice. A few close relations, and friends of the late Elvis also wrote their tributes, describing how they felt regarding his life and untimely passing. The tradition was that the eldest child in the family was going to stand in front of everyone during the burial ceremony to read out his tribute, which was already imprinted in the funeral brochure, as a way of giving the deceased a last honor.

Two days before the funeral ceremony, Elly stumbled on the printed brochures for the ceremony, flipped through the pages, saw all the tributes, and asked her mother why she wasn't informed about it as she would love to write a tribute for her father. Beatrice explained that she felt Elly was still young and might not be able to write fluently at that point. Elly was not happy with the explanation and felt offended that no one informed her to write a tribute to her late father, especially since they all knew the bond they shared while he was alive. She also found out that her elder brother was going to read his tribute during the ceremony, and she pleaded with her mother to allow her to join the brother.

Based on tradition only the eldest was expected to read out a tribute to the deceased in front of the crowd. However, her mother obliged her request, since she wanted to do everything within her power to make her daughter happy and not feel the absence of her father so much. Copies of the brochure had already been printed, so it meant Elly's name would not be included and shared with the guests. She decided to write hers down and read it out on that day.

On the funeral day, relatives, associates, colleagues and friends of both Beatrice and the late Elvis gathered to say their final goodbye to the fallen hero. His life was short-lived but impactful, as he left a legacy in the heart of his family, friends, colleagues, and students that he lectured. He had made a lot of impact through his spoken words and actions, including books published in his field of specialization which were used across several universities in the country. He was actively involved in a few charities and non-governmental organizations and made lots of positive impact in these institutions. He was also about to publish another book in his field of specialization before his untimely passing. Surely, the university where he lectured lost a rare gem, as he made a great deal of impact in the significant growth and recognition of the institution before his passing.

The funeral ceremony began, and a sense of calm filled the air, as everything unfolded smoothly. Throughout the chapel, many attendees wore solemn expressions, their sadness evident. Finally, it was time to read the tribute, and Elly stepped out alongside her eldest brother, both wearing black outfits, including a pair of dark shades worn by Tony. He didn't want to be seen crying while reading the tribute, since he maintained the mindset that men are expected to always be strong and not show any form of weakness—no matter the circumstance. He held his own life ideologies and was going to abide by them regardless of how others felt.

When Tony was done reading his tribute, it was Elly's turn to read hers, which she penned on the last page of one of the funeral brochures. Given her young age, it was written in simple terms, but one could easily tell the contents were straight from the heart. As she read aloud the tribute she had written she couldn't control her tears and wept bitterly as she continued to read them in front of the crowd. This turned out to be quite emotional, as almost everyone present cried either silently or was seen wiping tears off their cheeks. Her brother who stood beside her placed his hand across her shoulders and consoled her while she wept and read. At that point, even Tony could no longer hold back his own tears and allowed them to flow freely. "Oh, if only cries could bring the dead back," Elvis would have been back to life after that soul-touching tribute.

Also present at the funeral ceremony was her father's very close cousin, Dennis, who wept uncontrollably that day. Elvis and Dennis shared a special bond from childhood. Their mothers were sisters. Dennis, who was a kind and generous man, made a promise to Beatrice that he would not abandon her and the children and would help support them until they became financially independent.

He kept to his promise. This was unlike Elvis's brothers and sisters who seemed not to care about their late brother's family despite all he had done for them while he was alive, but rather turned their back on Beatrice and her children immediately after their brother's death. This hurt Beatrice deeply because she knew the extent to which her late husband supported his siblings while he was alive, including training most of them in school and a few to university level.

To worsen matters, some of them began fighting over some of the properties owned by Elvis and Beatrice, claiming that her late husband planned to give those properties to them before he died. Well, Beatrice, who knew they were lying, fought back and explained that her husband would have disclosed such intentions to her if they were true. She was certain that Elvis would never have hidden such information from her, as he loved her too much not to disclose such plans. Beatrice eventually won over her late husband's siblings since she was a very smart woman. This increased their hatred for her, and they avowed to never associate with her or her children, thereby making Elly and her siblings grow up without any connection to either their father's siblings or their children.

5 | FEAR AND HARASSMENT

Elly graduated high school with an average score. This was unusual for her. It felt as if her father's untimely passing continued to affect her even though she appeared to be happy most of the time. She often found it difficult to talk about her father because the memory always brought tears to her eyes. Whenever people who didn't know her well asked about her parents, she would redirect the conversation, avoiding any mention of her late father.

After graduating from high school, she had to work some hourly-paid jobs, alongside her two elder brothers, to help support their family, since their mother's monthly income was not sufficient for the family's upkeep. Elly was known to be extremely hard working, putting in her best effort to ensure every task she worked on was properly executed. Beatrice, seeing how industrious her daughter was at that age, decided to encourage and appreciate her by enrolling her in a computer school to expand her skill sets further.

From a young age, Elly exhibited a natural talent for computer systems and quickly acquired the basic skills. Impressed by her enthusiasm, Elvis decided to purchase a desktop computer for the whole family, using it as a tool to teach Elly and her siblings the fundamental uses and functions. Moreover, they were introduced to the world of coding at an early age by their late father.

Beatrice's friend owned about eight computer centers and had over 25 employees working for him in various locations. Through these computer centers they provided computer training including typing lessons and use of some advanced computer functions and certain software to various people. This was a means of equipping the younger generation with information technology skills given the world was shifting to technology. It felt like anyone without information technology skills was missing out on a vital aspect of the world's dynamics, hence there was increasing adoption of the skills. The computer center also provided certain other services to customers such as printing, laminating and photocopying of documents, and seemed to be expanding quite well due to the business strategies adopted by the founder.

Beatrice's request to accommodate her daughter in the computer training program was honored by her friend. They shared a close relationship back in the days when they attended the same university and agreed to maintain a cordial relationship until graduation. Their decision to remain just friends at the time was to avoid any form of distractions towards their education. This was of utmost importance to them as they needed to graduate with perfect grades. After graduation, he asked Beatrice out on a proper date which she accepted, and subsequently they began dating.

Four years later he asked Beatrice to marry him, and she accepted his proposal. Unfortunately, they were unable to proceed with the marriage plans due to genotype issues. When they realized the incompatibility with their genotypes, they were heartbroken, as they were very fond of each other. At first, they decided to move ahead with their plans, believing they would handle whatever issues might have arisen in the future from this decision.

Eventually, they ended the engagement and counted their losses, as Beatrice was reminded of a close relative whose son suffered much as a child from sickle cell disease. As she remembered the painful ordeal, she realized that she couldn't knowingly allow any of her children to experience such turmoil in life. She would never forgive herself if her children had to endure that level of pain.

The boy's parents who got married without checking their genotype compatibility realized the mistake after marriage, when the child fell sick frequently. The rate at which the child fell ill was worrisome to the couple who visited several hospitals to understand the reason behind the constant sickness. Eventually after a series of tests and hospital visitation, the root cause of the ailment was discovered. The child was suffering from sickle cell disease. The doctor explained this to the couple and enquired from them if they checked their genotypes to ensure compatibility before getting married. The parents who did not seem to understand the essence and benefits of genotype compatibility were at that point educated by the doctor, but it was too late since the mistake had been made. The couple explained that no one had advised them to run such tests prior to the wedding, and they felt so sad that they were the cause of their child's frequent pains, though unknowingly.

Beatrice remembered how this affected the family whenever their child had frequent episodes and had to be admitted for days in the hospital until he got better and discharged. The child endured so much pain till the age of seven, when he finally passed away from this same disease. The family was torn apart because of his death and the parents eventually separated as they didn't seem to get over the loss of their child. Beatrice felt it wasn't worth risking the lives of her unborn children, just because they were in love with each other. They amicably separated and agreed to just remain friends, which they seemed to maintain and remained cordial with each other. Their level of interaction reduced significantly after Beatrice met and married Elvis.

Beatrice was able to secure the opportunity for her daughter through her friend, and Elly was glad that there was an opportunity to improve her computer skills further. Beatrice's friend agreed to allow Elly to attend his computer training center and learn all necessary skills at no cost. He proceeded to introduce her to the overall supervisor of the centers who was going to be responsible for her well-being and ensure she got the required training. They agreed she will be at the head office twice a week to learn and help with other services provided at the location.

Elly quickly started her computer lessons and was enjoying the experience. However, her enjoyment was interrupted when the supervisor, who was supposed to ensure her well-being, began making inappropriate advances towards her. She was amazed and wondered how a man who was old enough to be her father could develop such unhealthy feelings and harass her in that manner. She decided to ignore him and focus her attention on what she was there to learn.

Days went by, and she continued ignoring him, continued learning and gathering the necessary computer skills. On a fateful day, as Elly passed his office, he called her into the office and asked her to have a seat beside him. He proceeded to ask about her well-being and if she was settling well in the office. As he was asking these questions, and acting like he cared about her wellbeing, he started touching the hairs on her legs, while his hand kept going up towards her lap. Elly sat there for a while, wondering what was happening since she had never been in that position before. She couldn't seem to understand what was happening, but she knew it wasn't right as she was feeling very uncomfortable with the way he touched and looked at her. As he noticed she was becoming uneasy with the way he kept touching her, he tried to calm her down by assuring her that what he was doing was harmless, and he just wanted to make her feel like the beautiful lady that she was. "You will be grateful to me by the time I'm through" he said. It was obvious he was trying to take advantage of her innocence.

He continued touching her legs and laps inappropriately until Elly suddenly screamed and ran to the door, opened it, and fled from the office. The staff and other people present saw how she ran out and looked at him awkwardly. He screamed at them to get back to work, "there is nothing to see here" he shouted. Some of the staff already knew what might have transpired behind the closed door, since they were aware of his lifestyle and past record of harassing the female employees'. They went back to work, choosing not to speak about the incident since he was the boss. They stared at each other, shook their heads in disbelief, and continued their work.

Elly, who was shaking when she returned home, thought of reporting the incident to her mother, but on a second whim decided to remain quiet about it, as she wasn't sure how her mother would react. She, however, continued going to the office on the agreed days, to learn and help where needed, but had made up her mind never to enter the man's office—for anything—not even when he called her into the room to give her any form of work instructions. She resisted all his advances and continued to acquire all the knowledge she could. "It is going to be difficult for him to ask me to stop visiting the computer center since I'm there at the owner's request," Elly muttered to herself. She was going to avoid him as much as possible.

He became angry with Elly when he noticed how she avoided him in the office. Since he was unable to ask her to stop attending the training due to her mother's relationship with the founder, he decided to make life unbearable for her. He had also threatened her regarding exposing what transpired between them, hence Elly was too scared to tell anyone what she was experiencing.

Days went by, and he felt she was not feeling the impact of his actions towards her so he decided to exert more pressure. He stopped her from learning any computer skills but continued to use her for other services provided at the center without any form of payment. This was designed to frustrate and make her leave on her own accord since he didn't have the power to do so.

Eventually, Elly decided to stop attending since she wasn't learning anything and wasn't paid for other services provided to customers. She told her mother about her decision to stop attending the computer classes and Beatrice was surprised at the decision. She couldn't seem to understand why Elly made that decision, and the excuses she gave were all very vague. It seemed like the threats from the man instilled so much fear into her, hence she was not willing to tell her mother what had transpired.

Beatrice, who was surprised about this decision, felt in her spirit that there was more to the story. The reasons her daughter gave didn't seem to add up and she was determined to get some answers. She knew how passionate and excited her daughter was when she commenced the lessons. Elly had shown so much enthusiasm when she secured the opportunity for her. As she thought more on their earlier conversation, when Elly informed her of her decision to quit, she recalled how over the past few days Elly's initial excitement seemed to have faded away. She remembered that some days Elly acted reluctant to attend the lessons. A cloud of thoughts enveloped her mind, and she knew something was wrong. There was more to this rash decision.

Beatrice decided to probe her daughter further to get to the root of the matter. As she kept probing, Elly insisted that nothing was wrong. She simply stated that she was no longer interested in the computer classes. She tried to convince her mother that she was telling the truth, but Beatrice noticed that she avoided her gaze while speaking, probably to avoid her noticing the tears that formed in her eyes. This bothered Beatrice for some days, and she wondered why her daughter was not comfortable enough to confide in her. She could tell from their earlier discussions that she was hiding something from her, but she didn't want to make any assumptions without fully knowing what the real issue was.

One night, Beatrice found herself unable to sleep due to this matter. She tossed and turned in her bed, unable to find peace. Filled with concern, she decided to get up and offer a heartfelt prayer, seeking guidance from God. She asked Him to help her find the right words to communicate with her daughter, so that she could encourage openness and address any troubles that may be weighing her down. She wanted to understand the main reason for the decision she took so she could guide her appropriately.

After the prayers, she proceeded to Elly's room to wake her up, and requested to have a quiet conversation with her. Elly joined her mother in the living room a few minutes later. Beatrice calmly spoke to her daughter about this matter, promising that she was not going to react negatively if she talked to her about any challenges she was facing. "Why did you decide to quit the lessons?" She asked again calmly. "Please tell me the truth and I promise not to be angry nor harsh no matter how bad it is," she continued. Elly couldn't hold back her tears any longer and told her mother everything that had occurred.

She explained how he had threatened her, warning her not to disclose the incident to anyone. Beatrice consoled her daughter and assured her that no harm would come to her and that she would handle the matter. She praised her for not yielding to his advances and for standing her ground and explained that she was very proud of what she did.

Beatrice realized at that point that she was yet to educate her daughter on sex and decided to find a perfect day to enlighten her, so she would not fall prey and/or obtain misguided information from others. Beatrice reported the matter to her friend, since they had a good relationship and he assured her that the matter would be handled appropriately, to avoid others falling prey to such acts.

6 | LURED BY LIES

After the incident at the training center, Beatrice implored her daughter to remain at home and aid in the care of her younger siblings. This was due to her older sons already providing financial support, particularly Tony, her eldest son. The family received a reasonable income from their labor, which greatly alleviated their financial strain.

Beatrice believed that Elly was too young to be burdened with the family's financial troubles, thus she asked her to remain at home and tend to the younger ones instead. It was moments like these that she longed for her late husband the most, as she was dissatisfied with her children having to shoulder financial responsibilities at such a tender age. "They were meant to be exploring and savoring their teenage and adult years, not concerning themselves with finances during their youth," she often ruminated. "Well, life happens," she reflected.

Beatrice had the privilege of growing up in a lavish household, with her father being a highly esteemed businessman.

Their family's abundant wealth ensured that she and her siblings lacked nothing. They frequently embarked on exciting adventures, jet-setting across various countries during their extended vacations. As a result, they created countless cherished memories and had an absolute blast, savoring every moment of their youth. She often wished things were different for her children and they could have the kind of life she had growing up, but there was not much she could do; funds became limited after her husband passed away.

Elvis had invested a good amount of his earnings in the stock market when he was alive, so he had plenty of equity investments, but the stock market recently crashed, thereby rendering those investments useless. Her parents, whom she could count on to help her financially, were both dead, and no significant help seemed to be coming from anywhere. Her siblings had their own family issues to solve so they couldn't afford to help much. Her husband's siblings also didn't seem to care about her or even the children he left behind.

Sometimes she wondered how her late husband's siblings could be so cruel as to treat their own blood relatives without any care, especially since she knew how her husband catered to them while he was alive. "Even if they didn't care about her, what of the children? Shouldn't they be moved to pity that they were still very young and needed all the support they could get?" The only person who seemed to care about her and the children's well-being was her husband's cousin who promised to assist in his ability during the burial ceremony. Although he assisted financially on some occasions, including checking on them frequently, Beatrice understood that he had a lot of responsibilities, as he was also catering for the children of his immediate younger brother who had just passed. She decided not to bother him much with her own problem.

Tony was working with a car dealer at that point and made money from selling cars to customers. He was earning a good allowance from the company. Since he was such a smooth talker, he leveraged this to make regular sales and the owner of the car dealership loved him and gave him a good allowance for each car sold. Apart from the guaranteed hourly pay, he was frequently tipped by customers due to his conduct. He had a charming personality, and the customers loved the way he attended to them.

He realized how good he was at convincing people to buy cars from the dealership and considered owning a car dealership when he was much older and able to get start-up capital. His business model was going to be slightly different from the one operated at his current workplace, as he planned to have a short-term rental for luxury cars instead. He realized that most rich folks seemed to get bored easily with purchased cars and frequently wanted a change or upgrade. Since they often wanted something different, he felt there was no need for them to spend so much on an outright purchase. He would convince them to rent the car for a short-term instead. This offered them the opportunity to swap the car once they become bored with it and felt the need for a change. Also, based on a high-level analysis he performed, he realized that one could turnover a lot more profit via car rentals than from outright purchases. Although it seemed like a big task given his family background and the level of capital required, he held on to the power of hope and was certain that nothing would stop him from achieving what he had set his mind to do. Those who knew his late father well always mentioned how Tony reminded them of him, since he was strong-willed just like his father.

One aspect where he didn't resemble his father was in the aspect of love and faithfulness to a lady. Tony was known to be more of a "ladies' guy" as he developed a habit of going from one relationship to another, and his relationships never seemed to last more than a couple of weeks. He seemed to get bored easily and moved on from them rather quickly. His mother cautioned him regarding this lifestyle and tried to make him understand that it wasn't good to play with people's emotions that way. "You wouldn't be happy if your sisters were treated in a similar manner by men," Beatrice occasionally mentioned to him. All the advice and caution from his mother fell on deaf ears, as he failed to change his attitude towards relationships and ladies.

He was quite protective of his sisters, especially Elly since she was the prettiest of the two. He felt that every man who came close to them and wanted to either be friendly or go on a date was going to play with their feelings and treat them the way he did with other ladies. He never failed to remind them that he was the man of the house since their father had died and it was his responsibility to keep them safe, both physically and emotionally. Elly, who was already a teenager at the time, found his methods unfavorable and always complained about his attitude to their mother, who agreed with Tony, as she believed Elly was too young to handle such emotions.

Since Elly was beautiful, she frequently got attention from men but always turned them down once they approached her because of her brother's attitude and disapproval of such relationships. This seemed to be the case until she met Nate.

She bumped into Nate on her way back home from the food market to buy groceries for the family. She was walking home when Nate pulled up beside her with a car and asked to give her a ride to wherever she was going. She declined his request at first since she couldn't understand why such a young boy could be driving such a luxurious car. At that point, she didn't realize that Nate was from a wealthy home. His father owned a renowned real estate company in the country, and he made good money from the services rendered to customers.

As Nate kept pestering to give her a ride, she reluctantly accepted the offer since the walk back home was still far and the rays from the sun were hitting her hard. She prayed silently that no harm would come to her since she was in a stranger's car and her mother had warned her previously of such acts. He tried engaging her in discussions during the ride home, with the intention of getting to know her more, but Elly didn't say much, and only gave out her name and where she was headed. He realized she wasn't willing to give out details about herself during the ride and decided to keep quiet and just take her home.

When they were just a few blocks from the house, she asked him to stop the car, so she could walk the remaining distance home, since she didn't want anyone to see her getting out of his car. He waited in the car for a while and watched her walk away. He wanted to know the exact place where she lived, so he could try and get through to her. He was already smitten by Elly's beauty.

A couple of days passed by, and he summoned courage to visit her house, although he wasn't sure of the apartment number. He got to the gated apartment, looked around and fortunately for him, she was seated in front of the balcony and reading a book. He called her name and as she looked down and saw him, she was shocked, wondering what he was doing in her house uninvited. She went downstairs to meet him and ask what he was doing at her house. She asked him to please leave before someone saw him there. Nate explained that he couldn't seem to get her off his mind after they met a few days prior, so he decided to pay her a visit. Elly told him that she appreciated the ride home and insisted that he should leave immediately and not return. "I don't want any problems at home," she explained. "My brothers and mother are extremely strict and won't be happy if they see me talking to you or learn that you came to visit me" she continued.

Nate willingly agreed to depart, yet he expressed his undeniable commitment to return, displaying unwavering perseverance. He promptly reappeared the following day and subsequent days, refusing to surrender. His unwavering determination to capture her affection was evident, regardless of the means he employed. Since Elly wasn't giving him the time of day, he decided to change strategies and get close to her younger siblings instead. "I'm not here to see you" he jokingly told her one of the days he visited and proceeded to chat with her younger ones. They enjoyed his company as he played and joked around with them. Elly knew he was mischievous by that act and acted like she was not paying him any attention, but she realized that inwardly she was feeling fond of him. She noticed how gentle and soft spoken he was. He was also very handsome and charming, and frequently attracted the attention of ladies, which he turned down most times. He had developed some affections for Elly from the day he gave her a ride home and wasn't going to give up easily, especially since he had never felt this strongly about any lady before.

Elly eventually agreed to date Nate secretly without the knowledge of her mother and older siblings. He visited only when they were out of the house. Only her younger siblings were aware of the relationship, since they were always home. Elly and Nate pleaded with them to keep the affair a secret and Nate kept them happy and silent by bringing them certain confectioneries that they loved whenever he visited. This seemed to work and the affair remained a secret. They were able to hide it for close to three months before Tony found out.

He had been noticing some changes in Elly but couldn't figure out what it was until he stumbled upon one of the cards written by Nate, which contained a poem telling her how he felt. After reading the card, he thought about confronting her, but realizing that she might deny it, he decided to catch them in the act.

He wondered how long it might have been going on and was surprised they could hide it from him. The only explanation was that she was probably sneaking around with him whenever they were at work because that could be the only reason why he didn't know about the affair.

He asked one of his close friends to stay guard beside his house and watch out for this mysterious person his sister was dating. He asked him to inform him once he sees any unfamiliar face entering the house when he was away at work. "Also keep track of her movements whenever we are not at home," he told his friend. As usual, Nate showed up at the house after everyone left for work, and immediately Tony's friend alerted him.

He excused himself from work, citing a family emergency, and rushed back home to confront the person that his sister was having the affair with. He walked in and saw Nate with his hands on Elly's cheeks and she was grinning from one cheek to the other. He got furious and created a scene that left Elly embarrassed, before giving Nate a strict warning that he doesn't want to ever set his eyes on him again or see him anywhere near his sister. She became angry at her brother and shouted back, insisting that no one was ever going to separate them. Tony eventually walked Nate out of his house and warned him to stay away from his sister or face whatever consequences that might result from disobeying him.

Elly went into her room, locked the door, and cried and refused to leave the room until their mother returned. Beatrice got home late in the evening after a long day at work and was informed of what had transpired that day, and she sided with Tony, insisting that it was wrong that Elly kept such a secret from them. "It was wrong for you to sneak behind our backs with him and you are too young to get emotionally involved with any man" Beatrice cautioned her daughter. This didn't seem to go down well with Elly, who vowed that she was going to keep seeing him no matter how they felt about it, and no one was going to separate them.

Since Tony and her mother continued to make it difficult for them to see each other, Nate hatched a plan with Elly to run away from home and she agreed. Beatrice got home and realized that her daughter had packed a few things and left home, and she informed her two eldest sons of the recent development. Her decision to leave home didn't seem to come as a surprise to them because they knew she wasn't thinking straight anymore and was thinking with her heart. She had fallen in love with Nate, and women, even very intelligent ones, sometimes exercise poor judgment when it comes to matters of the heart.

When Elvis was alive, he frequently advised his children, particularly Elly, to forever shield their hearts and be careful with who they let in. "Emotional issues have a way of derailing people, thus you must always exercise care and wariness in selecting the company you keep. Remember, you can't choose your family, but you can certainly choose your friend or partner in life," he habitually imparted. Although he knew they were too young to understand what he said, he often felt strongly in his spirit to provide them with such words of advice. Also, he felt it was beneficial to instill the learning from their childhood, with the hope that they abide by it once they had grown older.

Tony, who had followed Nate secretly to his house prior to that day, went to his house in the company of his younger brother to find out if she was there or if his family knew of their whereabouts. Upon arriving at the house, they rang the doorbell. The housekeeper answered the door, before calling out to Nate's mother who was just getting in from the office. Tony and his brother explained the purpose of their visit to Nate's mother. She tried calling her son on the phone to confirm what was going on, but he didn't answer the call. Nate already knew that might happen, so he had agreed with Elly that none of them should answer any calls from anyone in their family. Nate's mother went to his bedroom to confirm if his clothing and other personal items were still there but found out that some of his belongings were gone, including a travel box they had just purchased for him, and confirmed the suspicion of the two boys. It was at that point she realized that his son had taken some money out of her closet, and she just shook her head in disbelief. She didn't seem very surprised, because she knew her son was capable of such acts, since she and her husband had spoiled him, given that he was their only son. They realized their mistake much later, after he grew older, and they had been seeking ways to make amends ever since. She joined Tony and his brother in the living room and advised them to go home and give it sometime, as teenagers often tend to pull such behaviors, but they always find their way back home.

It turned out that Nate's mother was right as Elly returned home two weeks afterwards. Although Beatrice was inwardly happy that her daughter was back home safely, she decided to punish her for running away. This was going to be a lesson for her and other siblings for future purposes. She wanted them to understand that it was unacceptable to run away from home no matter the disagreements. After such misbehavior, it is not expected of her to welcome them with open arms. She chose not to speak to Elly until she determined the most suitable punishment.

Elly troubled by her mother's silence continued to offer apologies. However, Beatrice remained indifferent to her pleas, and maintained her stonewalling. To make amends, Elly began displaying exemplary behavior at home, taking charge of cleaning and attending to errands. Additionally, she began volunteer work at a local shop. Recognizing how Nate caused numerous issues at home, she decided to end their relationship.

Beatrice noticed that her daughter had undergone a significant change and appeared genuinely remorseful. Realizing that she hadn't yet determined the most effective punishment, Beatrice decided to put an end to the silent treatment. Later that night, while everyone else slept, she called Elly into her room and spoke to her in a calm manner. Beatrice explained to Elly that her behavior was inappropriate and took the opportunity to offer her insight for future relationships. She emphasized the importance of timing in life and expressed her desire to protect Elly emotionally. "At this stage of your life you may not be able to handle emotional issues as they have a way of affecting people negatively when they occur," her mother advised. "Some people have lost it in life, due to emotional issues, and never find their way back," she explained. Elly, with her head bowed down and a remorseful countenance, apologized to her mother for her actions and promised not to get carried away by such affairs in the future.

Beatrice then asked her why she changed her mind and returned home. It was at this point that she explained to her mother how Nate had tried to force himself on her when they were away. She tried explaining to him that she was not ready for a sexual relationship, but he didn't want to listen, so she decided to leave him and go back home.

Beatrice heaved a sigh of relief after her daughter finished explaining and cautioned her further regarding relationships with men and which qualities to consider once she's mature enough. She thanked her mother for the advice and promised not to repeat the act again. She got up and walked away into her bedroom.

7 | UNFOLDING OF A LIFETIME OPPORTUNITY

Two years after completing high school, Elly decided to apply for admission to one of the country's prestigious universities. Due to financial struggles, she postponed taking the entrance exams right after graduation. Her mother pleaded with her to wait a while after graduation, to enable her to raise the necessary funds. Her immediate younger brother was already in the university, and she was attending to the educational needs of her younger siblings too.

Elly, who understood the financial difficulties facing her family at that point, accepted her mother's pleas. She understood her mother was really trying her best and it wasn't easy providing for that number of children and training them in school with her monthly earnings. Her mother had to take up additional work to make ends meet, but that still wasn't enough for the family. She considered her mother her hero, admiring her resilience and the way she rose to the challenge after their father's death. Her relentless effort in providing for her family and ensuring they acquired the right education was remarkable.

She had seen and heard of instances where some children had to drop out of school after their father's death, while some were sent to live with either relatives or other families since their mother could no longer cater for their needs. She had a friend from high school who was married a few months after they graduated, as the mother was no longer able to cater for her and the siblings after their father's death. The girl's mother arranged and married her off to the next available man whom she had no feelings for, and was much older than her, because the man promised to take care of the family's finances if he were allowed to marry the young girl. This is considered a form of child abuse, but the girl who had no choice, accepted to marry the man. Her mother explained that it was the only option for the family to survive, so she had no choice but to proceed with the marriage plans. The girl's mother lacked any skills to generate income, so staying at home to care for the children was the agreed arrangement between her and her late husband, with him being the sole financial provider. Now that he had passed away, she had no way of providing for her family financially.

Elly felt sorry for her friend when they met weeks after the wedding and she narrated her experience, including how the husband mistreated her in the marriage. As she listened to her friend speak, she realized that she might have been in the same position as her friend if not for her mother's determination.

Beatrice was approached by a young man who lived in the same neighborhood some weeks ago asking for Elly's hand in marriage. Just like her friend's mother, he had promised Beatrice that he would help the family financially and help train the other children if his marriage proposal was accepted. Her mother didn't even give the request a second thought but explained that her daughter was too young to be married to any man. She also gave the man a stern warning not to disturb her with such requests in the future.

Elly's respect for her mother increased after she left her friend's presence. She was grateful to her mother for not allowing her to become a victim of such circumstances. She promised herself to apply all the necessary effort in her education to ensure she graduated with outstanding scores and secured a great job, so she could assist her mother in training her younger siblings.

Their mother had informed them that no matter what it took, she would make sure they all attended the university, and explained to them that the only way they could show gratitude was by taking their education seriously. She made a promise to their late father before he died to ensure they all received a high level of university education, and she was going to keep it. She was certain that God would always make a way for her and provide the necessary resources. The only reason why anyone wouldn't get a university education was if they personally decided they were not interested, just like her first son who insisted that getting a university degree was not important to him and would rather venture into business full-time.

Tony dropped out of school after their father's death, as he felt there was no reason to be in school and waste any additional funds since he preferred having and managing his own business rather than obtaining a university degree. He explained to their mother that the only reason why he agreed to even attend in the first place was because of how strict their father was on education. Besides, he wasn't doing well in class, so there was no need to spend money to get a certificate he was not going to use in the future, he had explained.

Tony had a flare for business from a young age, and always saw himself owning his own business and becoming self-employed, which was unrelated to the course he was studying. Beatrice didn't like the idea of him dropping out of school, but she understood and allowed him to proceed with his decision, especially since she had a lot of financial obligations ahead. She had even stopped buying any dresses, shoes, or any luxury items for herself, but was saving up for her children's education.

The time finally came for Elly to write the entrance examinations, which was a key requirement for any university admissions. She dedicated herself to intense daily studying for the examinations because she aimed to achieve an outstanding score, which would ensure her admission into any school she desired. She was also working towards obtaining either a partially or fully funded scholarship in one of the top schools, as she knew that her mother would not be able to pay the entire tuition fee.

The entrance examination was a couple of months away and a prerequisite for registration was for each candidate to select two preferred courses, ranked as either first or second choice. Depending on the candidate's score and solely on the discretion of the university, the candidate gets offered either of these two courses. In some cases, the school can decide to decline both courses chosen by the candidate if the scores don't meet the cut-off mark, or they have reached the required quota for the session.

As she prepared for the entrance examination, she was confused on a preferred course of study as she had majored in pure sciences while in high school, rather than social sciences which was her preference. She had initially said she wanted to be an accountant. Her father, who was a brilliant science major and a physics professor, had advised her to consider venturing into the pure sciences field, rather than social sciences in high school. She agreed and shifted her interest to pure sciences based on her father's advice, because of the love she had for him. Now that her father was no longer alive to guide her, she was finding it difficult to decide which aspect of pure sciences to major in. She wept whenever she remembered that her father was never going to be there to guide her through such important decisions.

Her brothers, particularly Tony, often tried to assist and fill the vacuum left by their father, but unfortunately no one could ever take his place in her life. That void created could never be filled, but she had to find a way to move on, which she continually did, and it kept getting better with time. Her earnest desire was to always make him proud, and she was determined to do whatever it took to always make her father proud even though he was not physically present. She always had this mindset that her father was watching over her, siblings, and mother in the spirit. To her, this meant that he was also seeing how she was performing both in school and general life. So, she must always try to make him proud.

As she battled with the decision for course selection and didn't seem to be making any headway, she decided to ask her mother and immediate elder brother for assistance. The discussions with them didn't seem to be of much value to her, since she didn't seem to like any of the courses they suggested. Or probably she was unable to get clear details on how impactful or the future benefits from studying the suggested courses.

One of the key considerations for Elly in selecting any course of study was the prospects. She wanted to go into a field of study that afforded her higher chances of securing a great paying job after graduation. She saw how her mother struggled and worked multiple jobs to make ends meet, including the times she reached out to certain people for financial support. In some instances, she had seen her crying silently and could only imagine the level of stress she was going through. She felt pity for her mother that she had to go through all that and was determined to make it through the university with a perfect score, find a great job afterwards and help her as much as possible. As she tried to figure out a preferred course of study and it seemed like she was not making any headway, she decided to shift her mind towards other things, prayed about the decision, and believed that she would eventually make the right decision.

Three weeks afterwards, her eldest brother returned home, as he was working with a company in a different state at the time. They were all excited to see him since they hadn't seen him in a while. He informed only his immediate younger brother that he was going to be home on that day and asked him not to mention his planned arrival to anyone, particularly their mother, who tended to worry whenever any of her children traveled.

Beatrice developed a phobia for road travel during her adult years when a friend shared a story of her aunt that lost three children at the same time, while they journeyed back home from an event. The three boys left a birthday event thrown by a close friend and were speeding back home. Suddenly one of the car tires burst on the highway and since the person driving couldn't control the car anymore, the car somersaulted several times, before landing into a large ditch immediately killing all three occupants. The parents of these boys experienced so much anguish that they were never the same after losing three children on the same day. Her friend explained how her own parents decided after the incident not to allow any of their children to travel together, not even when they were going to similar places. They always had to enter different cars. This story caused Beatrice to develop some phobia regarding road travel, especially when traveling far.

Tony returned home that day and saw their mother in the

kitchen cooking. He tip-toed behind her, hugged and whispered into her ear saying, "I'm back." Beatrice, who was startled by the act, turned around, and seeing her son unexpectedly screamed for joy and hugged him affectionately. It almost felt like she knew that he would be home that day, as she was making one of Tony's favorite dishes. Although she and her son fought often, he was still her favorite child, as they seemed to have a deeper connection than the other children.

Beatrice and Tony had an unusual relationship, as they disagreed a lot when he was around, but whenever he traveled and was not home for a while, they became inseparable, always chatting over the phone. Despite their frequent disagreements, Tony never entertained any disrespect from anyone towards his mother, and that was the case from his childhood. He fought with one of his closest friends in the past over a rude remark made about his mother. The relationship with his mother continued to improve over the years as he matured and understood that no one could ever love him as much as his mother. She always had his back no matter the situation. Also, he realized that most of the things they fought about actually seemed quite trivial, so he tried as much as possible to avoid conflicts with her and found ways to express his love better, especially since he knew how much their father pampered her while he was still alive. She needed that kind of love and he tried to show her how much she meant to him most of the time.

Tony was warmly welcomed by everyone in the family, and after he chatted with them for a while, catching up on key things that happened while he was away, he went into the bedroom to unpack and bring out the items he had bought for each one. They expressed their gratitude for the gifts, and he watched with joy in his heart as they unwrapped the presents with much enthusiasm. He was pleased to see his family and happy they were all doing well.

The next day Tony was well rested, Elly went to meet him to discuss the difficulties she faced selecting an appropriate course of study. She was certain that her brother would provide her with the necessary guidance. In fact, she believed that God answered the prayers she made some weeks back, by bringing her brother home in an impromptu manner to guide her with this decision. Although Tony didn't like reading very much, he was a very wise person. Their father had said this a few times to Elly in the past. When Elvis was alive, he consistently told him that he was a smart and wise person, and if only he could settle down and take his studies seriously, the sky would be his starting point. Unfortunately, Tony always got carried away with too many playful acts as a young boy, making it difficult for him to settle down and read his books. He was fortunate enough to be smart and intelligent, with a retentive memory, so he whizzed through school examinations with what he retained during classes. He had no option but to stay quiet and listen to the teacher during classes or face severe punishments. He disliked punishments. He always looked forward to the break periods when the school bell rang. That was his favorite time in school, as that was the only period he could play with his friends. His father was concerned about his playful nature and tried all manner of things to get him to reduce the way he played. He scolded him often, but all his efforts seemed futile.

When he was about to enter high school, Elvis insisted he attend the military boarding school. Beatrice, who feared for her son's safety in such a school, pleaded with him to reconsider. Elvis stood by his decision, because he felt that if his son continued with that level of playfulness and stubbornness, he might never achieve anything meaningful in life. Though terrified, she reluctantly accepted, but explained that it was just going to be a trial period and for one school term. The outcome would determine if he continued with the school going forward. Beatrice always understood the benefit of having a united front towards raising their children, and always tried not to oppose her husband's views. One thing she never did was to argue with him in front of any of their children.

Tony eventually attended the military school and when he returned home at the end of the first year, she noticed some positive changes in him. He was calmer, though he still didn't like to read as much. As a result of the positive changes, she decided that it was probably best for him to complete his high school there.

Elly approached her brother and asked if she could discuss something with him. She explained that it was pertaining to electing a preferred course of study at the university. Tony looked at her, smiled, and responded that she was free to stop him anytime and anywhere to have any conversation, and he would always be available. She sat down beside him and explained the challenges she faced. She explained that she initially wanted to be an accountant, but with the pure science courses in high school, it's difficult to decide what she wants to be in the future "If only I know what I want to be in the future, it would make it easier to know which courses to study in the university," she explained to Tony. He listened to her speak without any interruptions and after she was done, he paused for a while and then explained to her that she shouldn't feel pressured about trying to figure out her life goals immediately. "It will surely become clearer with time," Tony explained. He went on to explain that "even if you select a course now and decide in future to switch to another field, you can always take the relevant classes or courses that will help with the switch. Nothing is cast in stone. There's a higher chance of career success in a field one is passionate about, but since you currently don't know what you are passionate about, let's approach this issue from the aspect of career prospects" he explained to Elly. As they discussed the prospect of various courses based on her interests, he helped her navigate through them, and they finally narrowed it down to two major courses – "Geology as first choice and Petroleum Engineering as second choice."

When they concluded, she felt satisfied about the choices she made and was happy that this issue was finally resolved. She was grateful to her brother for his help. Tony was pleased that he could guide her through it, as he always tried his best to fill the vacuum that their father had left behind, especially with his siblings. He was always happy whenever he made a fatherly impact in their lives and never failed to remind them that he always had their back. He often reminded his siblings of their father's regular advice to them when he was alive, which is "family is the most important relationship anyone can have. When all fails, your family will always be there to help you through life difficulties, and they should never take any one in the family for granted."

The entrance examinations took place a few weeks afterwards and as expected when the results were revealed, Elly scored high this meant she could pursue her first choice of study in the selected university, which ranked amongst the top 10 universities in their country. It was renowned for producing the best medical professionals and engineers in the country. The tuition fees were high, but she was hopeful that she would succeed in obtaining the scholarship she had applied for. The scholarship would cover more than half of the tuition fees, and her mother promised to raise funds for the balance. At the time Beatrice made the promise, she wasn't sure how the balance would be raised, but she was determined to raise the funds.

Elly prayed and waited patiently to receive the admissions letter from the school which would confirm details of her admission, including course of study, tuition, scholarship, and other useful information.

The admissions letter arrived one month after the results of the entrance examination were out and she joyfully opened it to see details of her admission. As she opened the letter and read the contents, her countenance fell, as the letter from the university showed that she was accepted, but only for her second choice of study, which was Petroleum engineering. Although she was excited that she got the admission, including a scholarship which covered more than half of her tuition fees, she wasn't entirely pleased that the school didn't offer her first choice.

The high score she made was supposed to guarantee her first choice. She researched more on her first choice of study– Geology, and for some reason she developed a surprising affinity for that subject. Although both courses she opted for shared similarities in terms of course programs, she realized from her research that Geology was a bit broader, and she didn't want to be limited to a particular sector, especially since she was yet to fully figure out her career goals.

Eventually, she cheered up, since it was still great news that she made it into a prestigious university, with a scholarship that helped to reduce the financial burden on her family. She also remembered her brother's advice about how she could make a switch if in the future she realized that she needed something different.

Her mother returned from work that day, and she ran to her and shared the good news. Beatrice danced for a while praising God for what he did for her family, particularly her daughter. Elly allowed her to finish with the jubilation before she proceeded to ask her mother for advice regarding the university offering her the second choice despite making an exceedingly high score.

Beatrice's advice to her was simple "do not bother yourself too much about things that seem out of your control, since most times things happen for a reason, and we don't often understand the reasons till sometime in the future." However, "if you feel strongly about the first choice you selected, you can also write to the school and confirm the possibility of switching courses since it might have been an oversight on their part," she advised her daughter. Beatrice concluded by saying, "but if you try and it doesn't work out the way you expect, trust that it's probably for the best." She reminded her of how she was initially confused when deciding on a preferred course of study and explained that it could mean that her path was being redirected.

Based on her mother's advice, she decided to write to the school stating her preferred course, explaining that she believed that with her high score on the examination the university should be able to give her an opportunity to study it. They responded days later, explaining that there were no more available slots for the course that session, since they had reached maximum capacity. They suggested that she could defer the admission to the next academic year, and she would be given high priority. Well, this was not an option for Elly after having stayed home for more than two years after her high school graduation. She responded back to the university confirming her acceptance of the course that was offered.

8 | BEAUTY AND BRAINS

After accepting the offer for a spot in the department, she began making necessary preparations to travel since the university was in a different state from where her family lived. She planned to travel the weekend prior to the date she was expected to commence the course registration process. As she prepared, her mother felt a bit sad that she was leaving home, since she had gotten used to seeing her every day.

She called her privately to give her words of advice regarding the journey ahead and advised her not to ever get carried away by activities in the university environment. A lot of students tend to get carried away with the numerous activities around campus and before they realize the impact on themselves and grades, it's often too late. Most people are also unable to remedy the impact. "You are there for only a few years and then you have the rest of your life to have fun, after you have made it through with very good grades and secured a wonderful job" she advised. "Remember where you are coming from, the morals instilled in you and how much we have struggled since your father passed, and don't bring any regrets to us and your late father's name" her mother continued.

Beatrice spoke to her daughter for a while, and as she was concluding her speech, tears formed in her eyes. She held back the tears, hugged her daughter, and told her that she would really miss her, but she knew in her spirit that this step was going to be the beginning of greater things for her life. Elly thanked her mother for the words of advice and promised to make her and the family proud and not to take the opportunity she was given for granted.

She finally traveled down to the university on the expected day. And on the first day of school resumption, she walked to her department for the course registrations and familiarized herself with the environment. The environment felt serene and she immediately loved the place. It felt like she was destined to be there. She interacted with some of her course mates; exchanging pleasantries.

As she chatted with some of the older students, they mentioned how the course was great but there was a particular lecturer who was renowned for harassing students sexually. She thought to herself that it wasn't enough that her first choice of study was denied by the university, now there could be a possibility of her being sexually harassed in the department. She decided not to think too much about what she just heard, but rather be positive and hope for a stress-free experience.

Lectures commenced a few days later. She had also finalized the registration process and was having a great time in the company of her peers. Since she was very intelligent, she got the attention of lecturers and other students. Just as expected, she also caught the attention of the lecturer they had warned her about, since she rarely entered a room unnoticed due to her astonishing beauty. However, he didn't bother Elly as much, since it seemed he was occupied with the other ladies who were basically throwing themselves at him. He had called her to his office a few times to chat in a friendly way and know some basic things about her, but that was the extent of their conversation, so far.

The first semester ended, and Elly did exceptionally well in all her courses and her lecturers were astonished at how well she had performed. Her overall score in the course taught by this lecturer was high, and none of the other students' scores came close to hers. He began to see her in a different light due to how exceptional she was. "This is real beauty with brains," he muttered to himself. The course was a tough one for students to grasp most of the time, so he was astonished at how well she had performed.

"This has never happened in the period of four years that he taught this subject to students," he said to his fellow lecturers. "In fact, to reduce the wide gap between her score and the next student's, I deducted some marks for every minor mistake she made." He explained that if he didn't take this approach, there would have been a widening gap in the students' scores, which was a bit shameful to him. He only made sure that her final score was still within the highest band, and that way it was still fair. This incident seemed to have completely changed how he saw Elly and the respect he had for her grew. He decided to have her only as a close friend, and nothing more.

Elly felt it was unwise to get too close to him especially with the way other female students always clustered around him. So, she stayed away and didn't get too close. He was handsome and young, so it didn't come as a surprise that he frequently got much attention from the female students. He also seemed to enjoy the attention he got.

Elly maintained a cordial relationship with her course mates and was liked by most of them for her simplicity and intelligence. They nominated her as their course representative, which she handled with much ease, without allowing the position to negatively impact her grades. She felt honored that her course mates found her worthy of representing them, and she was going to give it her best. However, she was unaware of some of the negative aspects of the role, mainly the exposure to some male lecturers in other departments, who seemed to have a reputation for sexually harassing female students. Had she understood this level of exposure, she would have reconsidered accepting the position.

She interacted with one of the lecturers on one occasion and noticed him making sexual advances at her. She was so disgusted with the situation that she angrily stormed out of his office. Here she was relieved that this lecturer in her department whom she thought would harass her eventually considered her as a friend but didn't realize that there were other men like that out there. She thought about not interacting with the man anymore since they were in different departments, but she realized that if she refused to interact with him, relevant information relating to the course handled by him might not get to her course mates, and she would break their trust. They trusted her enough to nominate her to represent them, and she wasn't going to let them down. She decided to speak with the lecturer in her department that she had a cordial relationship with, to inquire how to best deal with the situation.

As she narrated the encounter to him, he smiled, as if to say he already knows about the man and his escapades. "Well, I guess birds of a feather do flock together," she muttered to herself, as she waited to get the man's advice on how to handle the situation.

The man didn't say much to her, he took out his phone, placed it on speaker for her to hear, and then called him. After they exchanged pleasantries, he brought up the matter and explained to him that Elly was *his* girl, and he was considering having her as a wife. The lecturer explained that he wasn't aware of that fact, and since he had now brought it to his attention, he would not disturb her anymore. That was how she was freed from the harassment.

As the call ended, she burst with laughter and couldn't believe what had just transpired. They chatted for a while, and Elly thanked him for helping her out of the situation, stood up and left, all the while smiling as she couldn't believe how easily the matter was resolved.

This encounter brought Elly closer to him, and they maintained a friendly relationship throughout her stay in the university. Her closeness to the lecturer, however, seemed to have given a wrong impression to certain students, as a rumor ensued that she was one of his numerous girlfriends. Elly understood the relationship they had was nothing more than cordial, so she refused to be bothered by such rumors.

While attending university, she actively participated in several student and departmental organizations, where she held various leadership positions, including president, vice president, and secretary of several associations. She was renowned for her confident and articulate speech during meetings, fearlessly challenging decisions with wisdom and integrity.

Elly was often regarded as a beauty with brains, with most men seeking to be in a relationship with her, but she turned down most of the advances, explaining that she wanted to face her studies squarely and didn't want to entertain such distractions. Well, this seemed to be her principle and she followed through till her second year in the university when she met Richard who was persistent and finally swept her off her feet.

She agreed to date Richard but was unaware that he was regarded as a playboy and known to keep multiple relationships.

Women flocked to him due to his charisma. He also commanded respect and attention when he spoke. He was quite well-spoken.

Her relationship with Richard eventually became public knowledge, and a few people who knew his lifestyle and history with women tried to warn her, on several occasions, that dating him wasn't a good idea. She paid no attention to them. Well, there's a saying that "good girls often like bad boys," and it seemed like this was the case for her, as she had fallen deeply for him. Also, Richard loved and pampered her so much, making it all the more difficult for her to leave him or believe what she heard.

All seemed to be going fine with them until a year and half into the relationship when she caught him cheating with another lady. Previously, she had seen her boyfriend in the company of this lady, but he explained that they were just friends and occasionally studied together, since they were course mates. Some of Richard's close friends also gave her the same explanation when she asked them, so she felt a bit more convinced that it was true. They assured her of Richard's loyalty and told her not to worry about his friendship with the other lady. Richard had also introduced Elly to the lady as his girlfriend in the past, so she felt maybe there was really no need to worry and decided to ignore their friendship.

The day she caught them having an affair was on Richard's birthday, when she decided to pay him a surprise visit. Richard lived in a studio apartment outside of the university premises. On that fateful day, he told her that he was leaving town in the morning due to a family emergency and would return the following day. When he mentioned that, she was a bit unhappy since she was looking forward to spending his birthday with him, especially since he had thrown her a birthday party a few days prior.

Richard and Elly shared the same birth month, and he went all out during her birthday to make it memorable. He threw a birthday party for her, inviting friends from both sides and showered her with lots of gifts including a handmade card which had a picture of them together, since he had expressed his intentions of marrying her sometime in the future.

She accepted that he wasn't going to spend his birthday with her and decided to give him a birthday treat once returned.

However, during the evening of that day, she ran into one of Richard's friends outside the campus and while they were talking, his friend mentioned he was just returning from one of the bars, where he had a few drinks with Richard and some other friends to celebrate his birthday. She thought to herself that "maybe Richard probably came into town earlier than expected and forgot to inform her." She thought about the perfect gift to get him for his birthday, but since it was already late and she had limited funds, she couldn't decide on anything special at the time. After some thought, she finally decided to make him his favorite dish. She thought this was the perfect surprise since Richard always loved her food.

She went to the supermarket, got all the items needed to make his favorite dish, prepared it, and proceeded to Richard's house that night, in a bid to surprise her boyfriend. On getting there, she knocked on the door and heard him ask "who is at the door," but she maintained her silence. She stood a few meters away from the door, so that he wouldn't see her from the peephole. She knocked a second and third time and he gave the same response, but she kept mute and smiling, waiting for him to open the door and surprise him. Little did she know the reverse would be the case since she was about to receive the ultimate surprise from her boyfriend.

After knocking a few times without saying a word, Richard angrily opened the door, wanting to know who kept knocking at his door, refusing to utter a word even after he repeatedly asked.

He opened the door and saw Elly standing in front grinning from cheek to cheek, shouting "Surprise! Happy birthday." He smiled, but she noticed that he seemed a bit unsettled. She wasn't sure what was going on at that point and decided to have a look into his room. Since Richard lived in a studio apartment, it was easy to have a view of what was going on inside the apartment from the front door.

To her surprise, the same lady whom he claimed was just a friend, was lying on his bed covered with a duvet. She stood there for a few minutes, shifting her gaze intermittently between the lady and her boyfriend, who at this time had his head bowed down. He was also wearing only shorts, which she felt he must have just thrown on to answer the door. If he had known Elly was the one at the door, he probably would have found a better way to make the situation less embarrassing for all parties.

Since she didn't know what to say or how to react to the situation, she left the food at the entrance door and proceeded to walk away from the situation. She had initially planned to spend the night at Richard's, but at that moment all she could think about was how to leave that awkward moment.

Richard ran after her, pleading with her to forgive him, but she paid no attention and kept walking to the bus station to catch a bus back home. Since the weather was too cold, Richard felt like he was freezing and asked her to give him a few minutes to dress up properly and take her back home. He hurriedly ran back home, dressed up properly, and rushed out again to meet up with Elly but couldn't find her anymore. Elly couldn't bear to see him that night let alone walk with him after what just occurred, so she walked briskly to the bus station while he returned home to put on some decent clothes. Luckily, she got a bus immediately and proceeded to head back home.

Richard paced around for a while, hoping he would see her, but there was no sign of her. He went back home to try and reach her over the phone, since he rushed out of the house without his phone. He called repeatedly without any response, so he decided to rest the matter that night and try to find her the next day to apologize again. He was so disturbed throughout the night that he couldn't bear to look at the other lady, let alone touch her again, since his girlfriend, whom he loved very much, caught him in the act and there was no denying the affair.

When Elly arrived home, she sat on her bed for a while, as she tried to replay and process what she had just seen and realized that this was exactly what people were warning her about regarding Richard, but she never listened. She assumed that those men were just jealous, since some of them had previously asked her out. She had turned their requests down, explaining that she was not interested in a relationship at the time.

As she pondered the incident, she realized that no tears flowed down her eyes, and she wondered why she couldn't cry after what she witnessed. She seemed to be in shock, and it all felt like a bad dream, because she never believed that she could walk into such a sight or feel betrayed by someone she thought loved her so much. She wondered how long this was going on behind her back and how he could lie to her all this time, explaining that they were just friends, and even tried to cover up his deceit by introducing her to the lady as his girlfriend. All his close friends, those she considered to be her friends also deceived her, and they helped him make a fool of herself that night. She thought about the lady, and wondered if she had no shame, because she was aware of her relationship with Richard, but still allowed herself to be deceived into having an affair with him.

After she sat for a while, a flood of thoughts running through her head, she remembered how her brothers tried to protect her in the past, including when her mother mentioned that she was too young to handle such emotions, and then it dawned on her that this was what they were protecting her from.

Rather than cry after what she experienced, she braved up and decided to end things with her boyfriend. The trust in their relationship was broken. She wasn't going to maintain a relationship where trust was lacking, especially since she was aware of her tendency to over-analyze situations and was at times named an over-thinker. She genuinely loved Richard, but couldn't trust his loyalty anymore. And this meant that whenever they were apart, she would wonder if he was engaging another woman. "I'm not ready to entertain anything that will give me too much mental stress, so the best way forward is to end this relationship no matter how much I love him," she said. "It's better I end the relationship now, feel the pain for a while, cry if needed, than to go through the torture of always worrying and wondering what he might be doing at every point in time."

Richard had previously assured her that there was nothing to worry about regarding his closeness to the other lady. And at every point he said that it seemed so genuine. He always reassured her of his loyalty, which turned out to be untrue. For Elly, this incident changed everything about their relationship. This was a major lesson in how building and maintaining trust is vital in ensuring a healthy, successful, and long-lasting relationship. Once trust is broken it tends to affect every aspect of a relationship.

Fortunately for Elly, she was starting a six-month internship program with one of the international oil and gas companies in another state at the end of the semester, which was just a couple of weeks away. She knew that was a good opportunity for her to clear her head and move on from Richard, who was also expected to graduate during the period she was going to be away. It seemed like a relief for her, as she knew getting over him was going to be a bit tough due to the close relationship they shared.

Although she loved him, she knew it would be difficult to trust him again after what he had done, and since the trust was broken, there was no need to continue the relationship. What hurt her the most was the fact that she walked in on the sight of him cheating on her with the lady, and she couldn't seem to get the image out of her head.

Richard tried all possible ways to get her to speak with him, but wasn't successful, as she refused to speak with him or even see him. He was heartbroken for some time because he had lost the love of his life due to his mistakes, but eventually had to move on. Although they were still young and not ready to start a family together, he saw a future with Elly in it, but that seemed to have been ruined by his actions. He knew that no one could ever take her place in his heart, but he had to live with the consequences of his actions.

9 | SUCCESS MAKES A MERRY HEART

The six-month internship program with the new company commenced, and Elly remained hardworking, thus she eventually caught the attention of some of the top management staff. They discussed the possibility of returning to work with them after finalizing her university education. She was immensely excited and grateful to them. She managed to save up most of the funds she received from the company during her internship. She was aware of her mother's financial struggles and often wondered how she was still able to help pay her educational bills. Elly planned to use the money to settle some of her finances for the final year in the university, to help ease the burden for her mother.

At the end of the internship, she received notable feedback from her work supervisor. This not only helped her grades but also opened doors to further career conversations with the company post-graduation.

She returned to the university for the last hurdle, since that was her final year, and made up her mind not to be distracted by a relationship and instead resigned to focus squarely on her education—admitting to herself that the relationship with Richard had distracted her a bit. Richard called several times during her internship, but she refused to speak with him—she didn't want to rekindle the love that was between them. That was likely going to happen, since she still had some feelings for him. She decided not to allow herself to be that vulnerable again, especially since she didn't want any more distractions in her studies. Although Elly was a bit glad that there would be no more distractions since Richard had graduated and left the school, she also worried that she might have issues adjusting due to his absence. Aside from the betrayal, Richard cherished and pampered her so much during their relationship. The relationship had loads of good memories, and she feared that the school environment would always remind her of these fun times with Richard.

As she wondered and kept reminiscing on the good times with Richard, her thoughts immediately shifted to her family and the financial struggles they faced. It was a miracle that her mother was able to raise the additional funds needed for her education, hence she needed to make her mother proud and all the struggles count. She also remembered some of her late father's advice which was "Don't ever allow temporary pleasures derail you from lifetime opportunities. Always remember that life is a journey and there is time for everything." It was at this point that Elly realized she was focusing on the wrong things. Her focus should be on finding ways to suppress all the feelings she had for Richard and focus on her studies. Besides, she was due to graduate in less than one year and had all the time afterwards to reminisce on those feelings. She needed to focus all her energy towards ensuring she graduates with an excellent score, which will create room for enormous opportunities for her in the future. She had to make sure that the next few months counted.

Turns out that Elly's decision to channel all her energy into her studies eventually paid off, as her final year results turned out to be the best she ever had in the university. She got an excellent score for all the courses she took that year.

On the last day of the final exams, Elly and a few of her classmates threw a graduation party to mark their success in the university and they poured drinks on themselves, while they partied and danced till daybreak.

Finally, Elly arranged to travel back home and see her family as she hadn't seen them in a while. As she packed up her things, she paused for a while to take in some final moments in the university hostel and surroundings since she stayed in the hostel all through her university days, given that it was cheaper to live there. She was overjoyed that she made it through and was grateful that there were no outstanding financial payments due to be paid. During this period, she remembered her late father and wished he was alive to see how far she had succeeded and could only imagine how happy he would be to see her graduate from such a prestigious university, and with such excellent grades. She was grateful to her mother for weathering the hurdles with her, especially with the financial support, because she knew that it couldn't have been easy.

She made plans to travel back home in a few weeks to visit her family before the university's convocation ceremony which was scheduled to be held in a few months. As she was finalizing her clearance in the university, she received a call to meet with the university registrar for important information. She was troubled after receiving the call, because she wasn't informed of the purpose of the meeting. "Why are they asking to meet?" she wondered.

Lot of thoughts crossed her mind as she wondered why she was summoned. She finally calmed herself down and waited for the meeting to know its purpose, since she realized that worrying could not change a thing.

The day came, and she prayed silently, while she walked to the registrar's office for the meeting. Upon arrival she was ushered in by his secretary and she sat down curiously waiting to know why she had been summoned. She sat opposite the registrar, but noticed he kept a straight face, making it difficult to assess whether she was summoned for good or bad news. As he noticed that she felt uneasy and was shaking, probably out of fear, he smiled and told her to relax, that the meeting was for good news, not the opposite.

On hearing that, Elly relaxed a bit and waited to hear the news. He started speaking but was interrupted by a knock on his door. He paused for a moment and excused himself to find out who was at the door. He stepped out of the office briefly and returned a few minutes later to continue the conversation. He eventually broke the good news to Elly, that she was chosen as the school valedictorian for that academic session. When she heard the news, she didn't seem to understand at first, as she assumed he was referring to the best graduating student in her department. She repeated what the man had said, as if to clarify her understanding, and the man nodded in affirmation and she kept looking at him, trying to process what she had heard. She couldn't understand how she turned out to be the overall best student for an entire school, which from her quick assessment had over 5,000 people graduating during that session.

When she finally got her voice back, she thanked the man, and asked what the next steps were. He explained that she would be contacted again within the next few weeks to explain further. He could see that she was still shocked by the news and told her to take some time to process it, and she could leave the office whenever she was ready.

She eventually got up and walked back to the school hostel. She cried for a while since she had mixed feelings. She was overjoyed because of this outstanding achievement, but a bit unhappy that her father was not there to celebrate with her. She could only imagine how happy he would be upon hearing such news.

As she finalized her clearance and there was nothing left for her to do in the university, she decided to travel back home, with the hope of returning to the university in a few months for the convocation ceremony. She also wanted to get home and share the great news with her family, since she was yet to tell them. She deliberately decided not to mention that over the phone, since she wanted to see the joy in their faces on hearing the news.

When Beatrice saw her daughter, she hugged her affectionately, since she hadn't seen her since the beginning of her final year in the university. She immediately proceeded to prepare one of her favorite dishes. Her siblings who were home at the time also welcomed her warmly and they all sat together to exchange pleasantries, catching up on past events and laughing affectionately. Elly gave them details of all that ocuurred while she was at the university and told them about her experience with Richard. At this point, she was no longer hurting from the betrayal, so she laughed heartily about the incident along with her siblings. Due to the loud laughter, their mother came out of the kitchen to find out why they were laughing so loudly, but they unanimously said "nothing," as she hissed and walked away. They were not ready for a lecture that evening regarding men, so no one was willing to tell her the story.

Beatrice finished preparing dinner for her family and they all gathered round the dining table and ate in silence, due to their mother's dinner rule of "no talking while eating." They maintained this tradition from childhood.

Once everyone finished eating, they thanked their mother for the food, cleared the plates and then Elly cleared her throat and said she had news to share, which she wanted to share when they were all together. They all sat silently waiting for the news and then she looked down and said, "I'm pregnant." She went on to explain that she was planning to move in with her boyfriend, so they could start a family together.

She lifted her face again to gauge the reaction from her family, and as she noticed the confusion on their faces, she burst out laughing and explained that she was just pulling their legs. She then informed them of the great news, that she was the school's valedictorian. She went on to explain what this meant to the benefit of her younger ones who might not have understood. "This is an award given to the student with the highest overall grade, having an outstanding performance in the entire university for the graduating session, and will be presented during the next convocation ceremony," she explained. Her mother and siblings screeched with joy as they heard the news.

Beatrice, singing and dancing as she celebrated with her family, went inside and brought out an expensive fruity wine that was usually reserved for important guests and asked them to bring out the wine glasses, as the news called for a celebration. After they had the wine and everything was calm, she noticed that her mother was suddenly quiet and gazing into an empty space, and she could already tell what was going through her mind. Elly went over to where she was seated, placed her hand across her neck and said, "Yes, I'm sure he is also very proud of me," and walked to her bedroom, laid down, covered herself, and slept.

Beatrice barely slept that night because of the great news and was grateful to God for helping her raise the funds needed to train her daughter through the university. She remembered how fearful she was when Elly informed her of the significant amount of additional funding required...which exceeded the scholarship. But eventually they made it through. She came to more profoundly appreciate the sentiment, "the journey of a thousand miles begins with one step."

The day of the convocation ceremony finally arrived, and Elly traveled to the university, accompanied by her mother and two younger siblings. As the school valedictorian, she was required to give a speech on behalf of the students graduating that academic year. She wrote her speech down prior to the ceremony and it was reviewed by the relevant people at the university. She sat on the podium with other students who had distinguished themselves in various fields, including dignitaries from the state, such as the state governor, vice chancellor and other prominent individuals. They all congratulated her on her outstanding performance.

The time for the speech approached and she walked gallantly to the microphone to address the crowd. Just as she was about to start reading the speech, she heard someone from behind her shouting "that's my daughter." She wondered what was happening and as she turned back, she noticed that her mother had left the guests arena and wanted to join the section where the dignitaries were seated. The security team tried to stop her from gaining access, since it was a reserved section, and that was when she tried to make them understand Elly was her daughter. The security detectives eventually allowed her to sit close to the podium when they realized who she was.

Beatrice, proud of her daughter, gazed at her with much admiration and joy in her heart, as she read her speech, collected her certificates, and took pictures with dignitaries and the other awardees. As she glanced upon her daughter, she suddenly remembered her late husband once again and her countenance saddened, as she wished he were alive to witness this landmark achievement of their daughter. She could only imagine the depth of his joy. She eventually decided to let go of the feelings, as she held back the tears that were beginning to form in her eyes, and rather shifted her focus to the present reality and to celebrating her daughter's outstanding achievement.

10 | THE REWARD OF RESOLVE

As a result of Elly's achievements, she gained the attention of certain noteworthy organizations. Several delegates from these organizations graced the convocation ceremony in order to acquaint themselves with the graduating class and scout potential candidates for specific employment openings. The ceremony provided students with excellent opportunities to secure promising job offers. The university consistently witnessed arrivals of representatives from reputable companies during the event, as its reputation for nurturing accomplished individuals who meet industry benchmarks was well-known.

Elly was approached by individuals from three companies, including recruiters who were interested in discussing possible job opportunities. They exchanged contact information with her and explained they would be in touch over the next few weeks to discuss further. She thanked them for considering her for such opportunities and proceeded to go home with her mother.

Beatrice, proud of her daughter, smiled often on the ride home, while repeating how proud she was of her performance and achievements. She assured her daughter that she was sure her father was very proud of her, even though he was no longer with them. Beatrice was grateful that she was able to provide her daughter a quality level university experience. Although raising the funds used to support her throughout the period of her education was not any easy task. Now that her daughter was out of university and she had great prospects in terms of a good job, she could have some breathing space in terms of finances, and she could also help her train the younger ones. Elly, just like her late father, demonstrated a kind and generous heart, always willing to assist others to the best of her ability.

A few weeks went by, and two of the companies, which were global international oil and gas companies, reached out to Elly, as promised. They invited her to their offices to discuss opportunities, including interviewing her briefly to assess her fit for the graduate positions, which they were looking to fill. She conversed with them and asked a few questions to gain an understanding of the roles. After the discussions and interview, she returned home. They explained that her job offer letters would be sent by e-mail.

A week after the conversations and short interview, she received a job offer letter from one of the companies, which contained details of her employment and how much she would earn on an annual basis.

The day she received the offer letter, she was home, chatting with her mother and siblings after having lunch, when the e-mail dropped on her phone. She looked at the name of the sender and title, and realized it was the offer letter and proceeded to download and open the attached file. She opened the attachment and scrolled through the document until she got to the section that contained the remuneration package.

As she saw the stated total annual pay, she froze for a while as she could not believe the amount that was included in her annual remuneration package. She expected that after graduation, she would land a good paying job and things would be financially better for her and the family, but she didn't expect to see such a generous salary, and especially not as her first job. She remained mute while she was in total shock, she kept looking at the figure, as she couldn't seem to reconcile what she was reading.

Suddenly, she got up and threw her phone on the chair and started screaming for joy, to the surprise of her family. Her mother realized that it was probably great news, suspecting it was related to the job interview she traveled to attend a few days before. She picked up the phone, and as she saw the amount stated on the job offer letter, she leaped for joy and rejoiced with her daughter, as joyous tears flowed through her eyes. She had really struggled financially ever since her husband's passing, and this was more than a big relief for her and the family.

For a while they sat, just staring at each other, wondering what was happening, and it almost seemed like a dream to them. Her siblings weren't left out in the joy, as they were very happy for their sister and started compiling a list of what they wanted her to get for them once she gets her first salary. Elly just shook her head when they said that, but she responded saying "I'm more than capable to handle these requests and will ensure all of you are well taken care of henceforth." For Elly, her mother was going to be her main priority, as she would make sure she did not have to stress herself for anything anymore. It was now time for her to enjoy the fruit of her labor.

The next day, she received a second job offer letter from another company she had interviewed with, and though the annual pay was also high, it was a few thousand higher than the first one. This time she wasn't as shocked as the previous day. Since she had to decide and accept only one of the job offers, she decided to accept the one with the highest remuneration package, because they were both renowned firms within the petroleum sector. Due to lack of experience in the corporate world, and no mentors to guide her, she failed to realize that other than the annual pay, other factors such as organizational culture should be considered when making such decisions, especially since they offered similar packages. She responded to both emails appropriately, rejecting the first offer and accepting the second one.

The employment start date was also agreed upon with the preferred company—which was in one month's time. She was also informed that a relocation allowance would be allotted since she was moving to a different state for work. This meant that she would be leaving her mother and siblings behind to commence work. For Elly, relocating was not a big deal, since she had grown used to being away from her mother and siblings. They could always come and visit her when needed. And with her salary, she could afford to fly them to visit her as often as needed.

She finally uprooted and moved to the city where her new office was located and was welcomed warmly by her colleagues. She was informed that the staff recruitment training for the new role would take place overseas and would be held in a few weeks' time. Necessary preparations were carried out by the company to enable them to travel for the training. This would be Elly's first overseas trip. She was over-joyed as she looked forward to the training and particularly the trip. She heard, watched on television, and read a lot about life in different countries, and embraced the opportunity to experience different environments and cultures. She felt as if her life were about to take an entirely new direction and still other times it all felt like a dream. She hadn't fully come to terms with her success, especially knowing how her family struggled after the death of their father.

She spoke with her mother regularly over the phone and updated her on how she was settling in, including the planned overseas trip and her experiences at work. Her mother was happy that she was settling well.

After the travel arrangements were finalized, Elly traveled overseas for a three-weeks training period and ensured she explored major parts of the Vatican City with her colleagues. She didn't take many pictures, since she wasn't the type to take regular pictures. The few pictures she took were because she wanted memories of the first time she traveled overseas. Her mother and especially siblings also requested pictures and videos of the country.

During the training, she participated and was noticed by the trainers due to how she answered questions, including contributions made during the training. After the three-weeks period of training, she returned home with her colleagues and resumed working in the office, with each assigned to respective teams and introduced to the supervisors for the teams. She bonded well with her colleagues and asked questions regularly as she familiarized herself with the new environment.

Things seemed to be going well, until the supervisor in the unit she was assigned to started making sexual advances at her. She remembered her experience with the supervisor in the computer center where she worked some years back and felt unhappy that this was happening to her again. She wondered if it was a crime to be beautiful, since all she wanted was to be recognized for her contributions and hard work. She wanted her promotions and achievements to always be based on merit and performance, not because she was involved with any man.

Elly considered herself a go-getter, and on a few occasions when she was asked to describe the type of animal she could be likened to, she cited the "Eagle" because she was going to soar to greater heights. All these unnecessary disturbances from men were not what she wanted, especially since some of them were almost old enough to be her father.

Elly was sure that she was never going to yield to the sexual advances from her team supervisor, but she was a bit bothered because she was not sure how this would affect her at work, including any future promotions. He was responsible for her performance ratings, which means that whatever feedback he provided regarding her performance at work determined how quickly she moved to the next level in the company. She discussed the issue with her mother during one of their frequent chats, and she counseled her to continue working hard, resist whatever advances he made and remain in prayer about it. Beatrice assured her daughter that everything would work out for the best. She also shared a story of her former friend who encountered similar issues from her superior at work, and how she prayed and trusted God, while she constantly resisted the man's advances. The man frustrated her at work for over a year, and she reported the matter to their main supervisor who did nothing, since he had a close relationship with this man. They were in a similar club, where they played golf and other sports together. Her friend endured the harassment and kept her head high, as she refused to be broken by the circumstances, but prayed fervently for things to turn around for the better. Her prayers were answered, as the overall supervisor resigned and was replaced by another person who made life at work difficult for the man who was frustrating her. Eventually, he had to resign since he couldn't take the pressure anymore. Upon his resignation, her friend was asked to take over his position temporarily, while they searched for a replacement. In the process of searching for a good replacement, they noticed she was functioning quite well in that position and was formally offered the position with a significant pay increase.

As Elly listened to the story her mother told, she was strengthened, felt motivated, and decided from that point on not to be moved by any advances tossed at her by her team supervisor. She would remain firm, work hard, and pray continually about what she faced at work, believing that everything would turn around just like her mother's friend. She knew deep down that it might not be an easy task but was determined to push through the challenge and come out stronger and better. After all, "no good thing comes easy," she reminded herself.

Several months went by and the pressure at work continued, and she kept feeling harassed. On a few occasions, she considered resigning from the job, since it often felt like a lost cause. Some of her colleagues had also told her about how the man frustrated a few ladies out of the company in the past after they rejected his sexual advances. She sometimes wondered why a company with such good values which they communicate to internal and external stakeholders would condone such behavior. "Is it that they are not aware of this behavior?" she wondered. A few of the colleagues she spoke with regarding what she was facing mentioned that the man was known for making life miserable for women who refused or challenged him in the past, with some of them resigning when they couldn't take the pressure anymore. Those who tried to fight him by standing up to him or reporting to the relevant management team lost such battles, since he was well connected in the firm. "This means they are aware of these escapades," but why they were not willing to deal with it was something she couldn't comprehend.

The times she considered resigning from the firm, her mind always flashed back to her mother and siblings back home and wondered how they would cope without the financial assistance and stability she provided them. She didn't want them to go through any more financial struggles, especially her mother, so resigning was not an option. "I have to find another job before resigning from this," she assures herself. She remembered her mother's advice and story about her old friend, and decided to keep praying about the situation, keeping a positive spirit, while she searched for another job.

Several months passed, and the situation at work worsened, the work pressure increased daily, and she decided to take her one-month annual leave, with the intention of spending the period intensively searching for a new job. On the last day before she proceeded on her annual leave, she said a silent prayer before leaving, asking that the next time she set foot in the company, it will be to put in her resignation, as she hoped to get a better job offer during the leave.

About two weeks into her leave, she was invited by a friend to have dinner and drinks in a nice but expensive restaurant, and she accepted, even though she considered it an expensive venture. She thought of declining the request at first, but on second thought, she told herself that "with the hard work I put in over the past months, I deserve to have a treat and make myself happy." If she only knew that this decision was an answer to her prayers and a turning point for the issues she faced at work.

She arrived at the restaurant, and was having drinks and chatting with her friend, when a familiar face walked into the restaurant. And immediately she remembered where she had seen the face. It turned out to be one of the dignitaries from her state, who congratulated and spoke with her briefly during the university convocation ceremony. They had also taken pictures on that day. She excused herself from the table, walked over to where he was seated to greet him. He seemed to be waiting for someone to join him at the table. Elly introduced herself to him, and immediately he remembered her and the ceremony she mentioned. He asked her to sit for a while since the person he was meeting was yet to arrive. He asked about how she was faring and how life was treating her in general. Elly told him about how she got some job offers after graduation and the company she decided to work for. She told him about the challenge she was facing at work and how she needed help to get out of it. "The situation is really affecting me, and honestly, I took some time off work specifically because I need to search for another job. I don't have the luxury of resigning without another job offer given the financial status of my family," she explained. Elly, at this point, didn't know that the man she was pouring out her heart to had recently joined the company's board of directors, and the announcement was to be made in a couple of days. He was at the restaurant that day to meet with two of the top current board members who texted him that they were running a bit late due to traffic. He was going to order some drinks at the bar and wait for them before Elly walked up to him. The purpose of the meeting with the other members of the board was to finalize the terms of engagement prior to the announcement.

  He listened carefully as Elly talked about what she was going through at work and was saddened to learn about how people left the company because of such behavior. She was also plotting her exit. "Who knows the talents that this company may have lost because of this man's behavior," he wondered. He also couldn't seem to understand why such behavior was condoned. He immediately knew that this was the first thing he would address once the announcement was made. He was certain that this man she spoke about wasn't the only person getting away with such behavior, but he was going to be the scapegoat for others to learn.

Since it was not yet public knowledge that he was joining the board, he couldn't say much to Elly, but instead encouraged and admonished her, and assured her that everything was going to be alright and should reconsider her stance regarding leaving the company. His tone, as he assured her that the issue would be resolved soon, startled her a bit. She tried to probe further to understand the affirmative tone in which he spoke, but he refused to say anything further, and just gave out his call card that included his mobile number and asked her to give him a call in a few days' time, when things become clearer. As they concluded the conversation, Elly stood up and went to join her friend, while she continued to ponder over his comments in her head. Although she didn't seem to understand what he meant, she noticed that the anxiety she felt earlier regarding her annual leave ending in a couple of days without finding another job suddenly disappeared.

Her annual leave eventually came to an end, and she was due to resume back at work. Although it seemed like things didn't work out the way she thought and prayed, she didn't realize her prayers were already answered but in a different manner than she expected.

She returned to the office ready to confront whatever she met at work. Her colleagues welcomed her back, with one of them calling her aside to tell her about the latest development at work. She started with saying "my friend, you are free at last, no more harassment at work."

At first, Elly didn't quite understand what she was talking about and asked that she explain what she meant by that statement. Well, "a few days ago, the company announced the appointment of a new board member, who stated that he had heard rumors about sexual harassment in the workplace and his first task was to investigate these rumors and any one guilty of it will be dismissed immediately," her colleague explained. "Guess what? Our boss was indicted and was dismissed with immediate effect" she continued.

Elly was astonished when she heard the news and immediately remembered the man she met at the restaurant some days prior and the assurance he gave her that the issue would soon be resolved. She proceeded to ask the name of the newly appointed board member. Her colleague mentioned his name, and it turned out to be the same man she met that day. This was also the name on the call card he gave her. "Please can you repeat the name, I want to be sure I heard you clearly" Elly said. She repeated the same name.

Elly noticed she was trembling upon hearing the name and rushed to one of the bathrooms to calm herself down a bit. She didn't want to give any impression that she might have a hand in what just happened. Once she calmed down a bit, she called her mother and narrated the entire story, and Beatrice sang and danced, all the while praising God for helping and saving her daughter from the hands of such a man.

Elly pondered calling the man she met at the restaurant who helped her with this issue. She wasn't sure if she should call him due to his high rank in the company. She remembered his words that day at the restaurant, and how he gave out his personal mobile number to her and felt it might be appropriate to call him. She decided it was best to call him later in the evening after work. As she called and introduced herself, he responded immediately saying "I assured you everything was going to be settled and I'm certain that statement has now become clearer." Elly thanked him for helping her with the issue, but he responded saying "you owe no one, not even me an apology or appreciation, rather the company owes you and other victims an apology for failing to protect you all from such. He totally got what he deserved, so do not be sorry about anything."

The story of how her former supervisor was sacked spread like wildfire, and others engaging in similar activities in the company took caution and began to abstain from such acts. A new supervisor, this time a female, was eventually recruited to head the unit. Based on her appearance, one could assume she was a strict person. However, the reverse was the case, as she turned out to be kind, and gentle, and the team, including Elly, enjoyed working with her.

Elly learned a lot working with her, and with time she began to receive recognitions and awards for her contributions within the team. Her light, which was initially dimmed by her former boss, began to shine greatly as she quickly rose to higher ranks within the organization.

11 | THE NUANCES OF NAIVETY

Once her work-related issues were resolved, life pretty much returned to normal. Things were once again going smoothly for her, and she began dating a man, Gary whom she considered to be the love of her life. Gary was a tall, fair complexioned man who showered her with so much love and attention, and she fell in love with him. Unfortunately, she didn't realize at the time that he was a snake in the grass.

He concealed a vital part of himself from Elly, which was that he was already married with two kids, and his wife lived in a different state. He was able to hide this truth for a while because of the separate homes shared with his wife. It almost felt like the reason he chose to live separately was to have enough room to date other women. His wife was a stay-at-home mum based on their arrangement, so nothing prevented them from living in the same house. He had told his wife that due to the nature of his work, he would have to travel often, and employees are frequently moved to other office locations based on need. He wanted good stability for her and the children, so he suggested that it would be good if they had a permanent base, while he visited often. The wife agreed to the arrangement because it seemed reasonable to her. But this was not his true intention.

Elly, who didn't understand this level of deception, agreed to date him thinking the relationship had a future. The relationship was going well, and she felt so happy and loved by Gary, with some of her friends often commending how much Gary doted on her. Some had assured her that Gary was her "prince charming" with others playfully stating that they were going to commence wedding preparations ahead of his marriage proposal. Elly always laughed at these acts and comments from her friends, but inwardly she was pleased that she found a man that loved her as much as Gary did. If only she knew this was all an act wrapped in deceit, she would not have gotten carried away with his expressions of love. Indeed "not all that glitters is gold."

Eight months passed and the relationship continued to blossom till the deceit became exposed. Elly was relaxing on her sofa, scrolling through her phone, smiling as she read certain posts made by people on a social media platform when she suddenly stumbled onto one that had Gary's picture. She became curious and proceeded to read further. One of her connections had tagged Gary on a post, congratulating him on the birth of his third child. She was stunned on seeing the post and continued to look at it for a few minutes. For a moment she wondered if it was someone that looked just like Gary. But the picture and name were the same as Gary's, so this was no coincidence she thought to herself.

The social media handle in the tagged post was not one she was familiar with, which further increased her confusion at the time. Unknown to her, Gary had given her a different handle which had less activities and explained that he was not active on social media. She had believed him, since not everyone pays too much attention to social media, including her. Turns out that he purposely decided not to share his main handle with Elly because it contained pictures of his wife and children.

As Elly looked at the post and picture, she wondered for a while if this was really the man who had assured her of his intentions to marry her once he finalized his PhD program. She was dumbstruck as she continued to gaze at the picture and post, hoping it was all a dream. "Or could this be someone that has the same resemblance and name as Gary, she said aloud?" She was having trouble coming to terms with the fact that she had been deceived for such a length of time. She couldn't seem to believe that a man who professed love to her continuously would deceive her that way. There was nothing that showed he could possibly be married throughout the time she knew him.

As she pondered how to proceed with the information which had just come to light, she collected herself, summoned courage, and proceeded to view the profile page of the tagged post. She was initially scared to open it because she was afraid of finding out the truth. "How can I survive this betrayal, if it's true," she thought. As she attempted to view it, she noticed she was unable to access the page due to its privacy settings. She would have to be added to his friend's list to view the page or pictures. She couldn't request to be added in order to conceal that she was onto him.... in the event her suspicions were correct. She decided not to take any chances by raising any suspicions regarding what seemed like a hidden truth. She would not confront him without proof because he might deny it, even if it were true. Also, if her suspicions were unfounded, she didn't want to break his trust.

After pondering on this issue for a few days and wondering the best way forward, she decided to confide in one of her close friends, Stella, since when it comes to matters of the heart, people often throw caution to the wind and tend to exercise poor judgment. Stella opted to send a friend request to him on the social media platform using another account they had just opened, to avoid raising any suspicions. They waited to be granted access, which they received a few days later. As they scrolled through his page on the social media platform, they were astonished at what they saw. It turned out that her suspicions were not unfounded and the man she assumed was the love of her life was already married, and his wife had just given birth to their third child. This meant that he was probably on good terms with his wife, so one could rule out the possibility that they may be separated or having any significant marital issues.

As Elly looked at the pictures, she wept bitterly and lamented to her friend that she could not understand why she was so unlucky with men. She always fell for the wrong ones, despite how intelligent she was. Her friend consoled her and assured her that everything was going to be alright. Trust that someday the universe will connect you to your own "prince charming." "You only need to exercise a bit more patience and wait for the right time to come. People's destinies differ. While some tend to meet the right man without too much stress, others kiss many frogs before they find their own prince charming, and it has nothing to do with being intelligent," her friend advised. Although Elly found some comfort in the words of her friend, it didn't change the fact that she was heartbroken because of this revelation, and she wept for days.

Stella packed a few things and went to Elly's apartment to stay and comfort her. She felt it was not proper for her to be left alone in that state of mind. She could see how heartbroken she was and felt so much pity for her. She decided to stay with her friend until she felt better. She continued to console Elly, helping as much as possible to get her back on her feet again. However, she encouraged her to cry as much as she wanted, since it was just an emotion. "It's okay if all you need to do at this point is cry, just let it all out. I promise never to leave your side till you feel better," she told Elly.

During this period, Gary tried to reach her several times, but she refused to answer his calls. She was not ready to confront him with her recent findings. She thought to herself "He deceived me, and it was a deliberate act, so there's no point talking about it. He is only going to make excuses, and for her that was going to hurt more."

Gary decided to pay her a visit since she wasn't responding to his calls. He worried since he had called repeatedly over the past few days but received no response. Elly answered after an incessant door knocking session from him. Her eyes were swollen because she had been crying for a few days. She had also taken some time off work since she didn't want her colleagues to see her in that condition.

Gary walked into the apartment, asking what the issue was. "Why aren't you answering my calls, and why are your eyes so swollen?" Elly didn't say a word, but rather she took her phone and showed him some pictures with his family which they had gotten from his social media page. She continued to watch his reaction as he scrolled through the pictures on her phone.

At this point, Gary understood what was going on, and the only excuse he could give was that he failed to mention it because he was in love with her and didn't want to lose her because he was married. He went on for some minutes, trying to find ways to justify his actions, but no explanation was good enough for

Elly, who walked to the door, opened it and screamed at him to leave her house and never return. He hesitated for a while and seeing that she was certain about him leaving, walked out of the apartment as she shut the door behind him. He tried continually to reach her, sending messages and frequent apologies for his actions, but she was done with him and never replied to any of his calls and messages. Eventually, he could tell that she was done with him, and he decided to leave her alone.

A few weeks passed, and Elly was over him and the incident. She decided it was best to focus squarely on her career henceforth.

12 | CHOOSING FOR LIFE

After the several heartbreaks suffered at the hands of men, Elly decided not to involve herself in any long-term relationships. When she was ready for marriage, she would accept a marriage proposal from any man she felt attracted to. In addition, the man also must be gentle, kind, with other few attributes that she felt were important to her. It felt like she had given up on love due to her past failed relationships. "The love will come later in the marriage, only let him be kind and treat me right," she said to herself.

She stayed away from men and relationships till the age of 28, when she felt it was the right time to settle down and start a family. At this time, she had about three suitors and was confused as to the right person to choose. One major mistake she made during the selection process was she *judged a book by its cover* and failed to take time to study the men better and seek God's face concerning the suitors. She failed to realize that choosing a life partner was one of the most important decisions anyone can make in life. No matter how good a person is, if one chooses the wrong person, they can be doomed for life if not handled properly. Some people have lost their way in life and others suffered untimely deaths due to poor choices regarding relationships and marriage.

Elvis always cautioned his children about relationships and the importance of firmly guarding their hearts when he was alive. Due to how young they were at the time, they didn't seem to understand the advice he frequently gave, but he had assured them that it would get clearer as they got older. He spoke frequently about this important aspect of life and asked them to promise him to abide by it. It almost felt like he knew that he might not be around to guide them through such key decisions in life when they were of age.

Elvis grew up and saw how people's fortunes turned for the worse because of certain decisions made with regards to relationships and marriages, hence the need to prepare his children early enough.

In particular, he had a female colleague who previously worked with an international organization and rose to top ranks within the organization. She narrated her ordeal in the hands of her ex-husband, and he was moved to pity to hear all she had to endure. It happened that her ex-husband who was not doing very well in his business felt threatened by her promising career in the organization and asked her to resign and move over to the state where he was residing. They lived in different states due to her job. She refused initially, but as the man persisted and gave her an ultimatum to choose between the marriage and her job, she decided to resign from her job since she wanted to save her marriage and particularly image. She didn't want to be branded a failure in marriage. If only she confided in some good mentors, she might not have fallen victim to the husband's manipulations.

She eventually resigned based on the husband's wishes and joined him in the state where he was residing. She began to search for a new job since the organization did not have any office in that area. Also, the location where they now lived together was one of the remote areas in the country, so it wasn't easy to find a good job.

Weeks and months passed by, and she was unable to find a job and she had no regular income like before. Her husband was also not ready to provide for her financial needs and gave the bare minimum for house upkeep and meals. Gradually, the house became unsupportable for the couple and their only son, as they bickered every day and night due to financial challenges. They began to resent each other and with time they had to separate, and the marriage ended since they both couldn't withstand the financial pressure in the home. She moved out with her son from the matrimonial home and went back to the state where she was before, and tried to see if she could get her former job back. They informed her that her position was filled and there were no vacancies at the time. She felt saddened that she lost both a good job and her home, and wished the hands of the clock could be turned back so she could make a different decision. Since she could not get a similar job due to the high demand of such high paying jobs, she resorted to lecturing in the university, which was where she met the late Elvis.

Her story and some other similar stories relating to relationships that Elvis heard and witnessed often scared him as he watched his children grow. He silently hoped and wished that they would be a bit more cautious when it came to matters of the heart.

Elly had her fair share of heart breaks from men, and she had prayed that for all the disappointments and hurt that God would bless her with a man that would cherish her so much it would make her forget all the past hurts.

At this point in time, she decided it was right for her to be married. She had a few suitors and had to decide and choose one of them as her husband to be. She proceeded to choose a man that appeared so gentle, calm and looked like he couldn't hurt a fly. This was an attribute she always wanted in a man, but little did she know that the choice she was making would turn out to be her worst regret and nightmare in life.

One would wonder why someone as intelligent as Elly, who made such remarkable grades academically and was working with a renowned international oil and gas firm, accepted the marriage proposal from Donald, the chosen man, without carrying out proper due diligence. Well, it turned out that relationships were an area of weakness for Elly judging by her past struggles. She did not seem to make the best decisions when it came to men and relationships.

Donald, who was about six years older than Elly, was introduced to her by a close friend who portrayed an image of being a calm, quiet, and responsible man. After they were introduced, they scheduled a date for their first meeting at one of the restaurants in the city. They exchanged pleasantries and got to know each other a little bit. Her first impression of Donald seemed to be like the image of what was described, and she noticed how calm he was throughout their first date and how he made her laugh on a few occasions.

After their initial meeting, they continued to chat over the phone for long hours daily. They went on more dates and things were going very well, with feelings growing stronger with every passing day and he was very gentle with Elly.

Donald proposed less than four months after they met, explaining that he was certain she was the woman for him, so there was no need to waste any more time. Elly was a bit taken aback when he proposed since she felt it was too soon for a marriage proposal and requested some time to get back with a response. Although she had grown fond of him, she still wasn't sure about the decision to marry a man she had known for such a short time.

She decided to seek counsel from the close friend who introduced them. He advised Elly that she shouldn't be overly conscious of the timing of the courtship. In his view, "the length of time spent prior to getting married is not a factor for a successful or failed marriage." He explained that he had seen instances where marriages of couples who dated for several years fell apart just a few years into the marriage, and couples who didn't date up to one year lived happily for years after the marriage. He went on to tell her a story to buttress his point. I have a cousin who married her current husband within three months of being introduced by a close friend. Prior to them getting married, there was another man who kept asking for her hand in marriage for close to a year, and tried various ways to win her heart, but she refused his marriage proposal. When asked by her family why she continuously refused this man's proposal, she explained that she was certain in her spirit that he was not the right man for her. Whenever the man visited her father's house, she refused to see him despite her mother cautioning her and advising that she should give the man a chance. "Get to know him a little bit and if you still feel he isn't the man for you, we will respect your decision, her mother advised." She maintained her stance that she was not interested in him. All pleas and advice from her family, especially her mother regarding her refusal to give the man any chance fell on deaf ears. The man didn't give up and tried every means possible, including showing up with different types of cars, getting closer to her family to know if he could win her heart, but every request to have her as a wife failed.

A few months later, even while this man was still in the picture, and trying his best to win her heart, the lady was introduced to her current husband by a close friend. To everyone's surprise, after just a few dates, she accepted this man's marriage proposal. This proposal happened just two months after they first saw each other. Now the story gets better. The man whom she eventually accepted the marriage proposal from wasn't as wealthy as the first man, or so it seemed. But he was honest about the stage he was in and pleaded with her to stay by his side while they worked towards building the life of their dreams together. They eventually got married within less than three months of being introduced to each other. The wedding wasn't elaborate since he wasn't wealthy, but she was very happy with her decision and explained the same to her parents who were concerned that she accepted him over the other man who appeared to be the wealthier choice. To her, it seemed as if the material things that the man was throwing her way, including the way he changed cars just to impress her made her dislike him. She was never the type to care much about flamboyant lifestyles. Now the fortunate thing is that seven months into their marriage, the husband met a man who turned their life around drastically. They started a business partnership, and in a few years the business grew to become a national brand. "So, you see, not all that glitters is gold, and sometimes life takes an unprecedented turn." He further explained how the man adored his wife so much, despite not getting to know each other very well before the marriage. The couple have been happily married for over ten years' he said, as he concluded his story. "Well happiness is relative," Elly thought to herself, as she felt that he shouldn't conclude that the lady was happily married if he wasn't living with them.

Elly thanked him for the advice, but still wasn't certain about her response to Donald's marriage proposal, who by now was constantly asking for her response. She decided to also speak with one of her mentors about the matter who advised that "although he agrees that the length of time for courtship does not guarantee a successful marriage, time reveals most things." He encouraged her to consider giving up sometime before deciding on the marriage proposal.

Donald however, seemed to be putting her under a bit of pressure to respond to his request, explaining that the only reason he wanted it to happen so quickly was that his parents who reside outside of the country were coming home for another wedding ceremony of a very close relation and he wanted their wedding to coincide with theirs. He didn't want them to travel back and return in a few months only because of his wedding. Elly felt this was a good enough explanation and accepted his marriage proposal. She imagined that Donald, who seemed gentle and calm, would likely treat her like a queen but didn't realize that this was a masked identity.

After she accepted Donald's marriage proposal, he introduced her to his family who were based in a different country and hurriedly rushed through the wedding process, probably because he wanted to tie her down before she learned certain truths about him.

Meanwhile, as the wedding preparations were underway, one of her friends who was concerned about the hasty decision she was making, since she barely knew Donald, advised her to take some time to study and understand him to some extent before making such a decision. Elly argued that "there was no connection between the length of time spent during courtship and having a successful marriage," as statistics have shown that couples who also dated for an extended period also had failed marriages. "Well, that's true, her friend says, but time always reveals certain things about people." Elly seemed not to pay any attention to her friend and continued with the wedding plans.

As her friend noticed she was not paying any attention to what she was saying, she called her and said, "although I don't think it is a wise decision to marry this man that you barely know, I will respect your decision and provide support as much as possible." I became weary of appearances and learned not to judge circumstances based on appearances during my early teenage years after an experience with a close family member, her friend stated.

She began to narrate the encounter a close relation had with her ex-husband. She always adored their marriage, and, on a few occasions, she told her mother that she hoped to marry such a romantic man when she got older. Her mother, who felt that there was something more going on in the marriage than what was presented to the family, always cautioned her about such statements and told her to be careful with what she wished for. "Things are often not as they seem," said her mother. She was too naïve and inexperienced to understand what the mother was saying, but later understood when everything went sour. It turned out that this man who appeared to be nice and caring towards the woman whenever they visited her family turned out to be a thorn in the woman's flesh whenever they got home. The couple didn't have any child after six years of marriage and the man who was the only son of his family was taking out the frustration of the childlessness on the wife, even when several tests showed that there was nothing medically wrong with the woman. She endured the maltreatment and cried silently for a long time in the marriage and told no one about what she was going through until the man eventually threw her out of their home. At this point, he had gotten another lady pregnant and decided to bring her into his home. After she returned home to her family and narrated all she suffered in her marriage, most people were shocked since they could never have guessed that was happening from the way he acted lovingly towards her during their visits. "This was a turning experience in my life, and since then I learned never to judge people by their looks, as some people are truly wolves in sheep's clothing," she stated.

Elly was a bit moved by the story and for a moment she wondered if she was doing the right thing by marrying a man she barely knew, but as she remembered the story told by the friend who introduced Donald to her, she decided to proceed with her plans to marry him. If only Elly had listened to her friend and mentor and given the relationship a bit more time like they advised, she would have saved herself a lot of trouble, heartache and disappointments in the future. "How could she have known that this man who presented himself as an angel of light was going to be her worst nightmare."

13 | AN UNEXPECTED TURNAROUND

The wedding finally came to pass, and they settled into their new home. Elly held onto the hope that this would be the happily-ever-after she had dreamed of since her teenage years. During the initial months after the wedding, everything seemed to go smoothly. Donald exuded a calm and gentlemanly demeanor. However, after a couple of months she realized that his attitude towards her began to take a different turn and he turned into a completely different person from the man she met. This shouldn't have come as a total surprise because she barely knew him other than what he had presented, and she failed to find out if that was his true nature or just a facade.

She noticed Donald slowly withdrawing from her and refusing to participate in anything regarding the marriage. It felt as if he was uninterested in associating himself with her or the marriage, including attending events together, shopping, basically anything that a couple was meant to do together, he simply was not interested.

Elly found herself disturbed at the sudden turn of events and wondered why he acted indifferent towards her. She couldn't wrap her head around why he withdrew himself and on various occasions approached him to better understand what she might have done wrong or what she could do better.

On each occasion, there was never a reason provided regarding his sudden change of attitude, which left her all the more confused. All he offered was that "there were no issues and that he just wanted to be left alone." That response would not go down well with Elly who reminded him how important it is for them to engage in activities together to help create a lasting bond. "We need to be deliberate towards this marriage to ensure its success, especially since we didn't get the chance to know each other better before the marriage," Elly beckoned.

It appeared as if Donald took offense when she made mention of ensuring the success of their marriage, inquiring instead of why she was already thinking about the marriage failing. Elly further explained, "I'm not wishing for this marriage to fail, I want us to spend forever together, but rather I'm pointing out, given the way you have been acting, that I don't feel any connection towards you, and this is not good for any marriage. Marriage is like any other partnership which requires effort and contribution from both parties to ensure its success," she went on. "Our marriage will work, so speak positively always and stop thinking negatively," Donald grunted. She decided not to say anything more concerning the matter since he wasn't ready to listen.

What baffled Elly most times about Donald was how he was always full of positive words, speaking positively about circumstances but never backed any of it up with actions. "Faith without works is dead." How Donald expected their marriage to succeed with his nonchalant attitude seemed to baffle Elly, but she decided to speak and tread with caution in order to avoid coming off as a nagging woman.

She was at a loss on how to deal with the matter since several months passed and there were no obvious improvement at home. She thought about confiding in her mother and close friend but didn't want to seem like she was discussing her family issues with others. She also didn't want her mother to worry. She remembered how her close friend warned her about marrying a man whom she barely knew and felt it unwise to divulge what she was experiencing. She was afraid her friend might judge her, especially since she was the one to warn her about such a hasty decision.

Eventually and as a last resort, she summoned enough courage to discuss things with this particular friend since she deeply needed someone to confide in and to avoid sinking emotionally. Her friend felt pity for her upon hearing what she was going through. Although she wasn't surprised that things took a sudden turn, she still encouraged and promised to always be there for any support needed. Her advice to Elly was to have a conversation with Donald and find out what exactly the issue was. "Try to find out from him what you need to do for things to turn around, since communication is imperative to any relationship." Elly explained that she had asked him, but nothing seemed to be the matter. "Try harder." He needs to be open with you about what the issues are, because that's the first step towards understanding how to resolve the issue.

Elly decided to probe further based on her friend's advice, but it seemed like the constant questioning annoyed Donald who got irritated one of the days, pushed her aside while she hit her back against the wall and asked to be left alone. "I already told you that there are no issues, so stop bothering me," he said and proceeded to walk away from her. Elly followed him, "since you have made it clear that there are no issues, you need to understand that the way you are treating me and this marriage might affect us in the long run, please you need to do better," she pleaded. As she kept talking about the issue and how this might affect them in the long run if not properly addressed, Donald who was already irritated about the discussion yelled at her, asking once again to be left alone, and replied "I'm not interested in creating any bond with you, and if the marriage ends, then we will go our separate ways." Elly, shocked upon hearing such remarks, including some other unpleasant comments from him, decided not to speak about the matter any further and walked away to avoid any more escalations.

As she left his presence that fateful day, she felt restless and paced around the room, wondering what might have led to the change in his behavior. She kept thinking back to know if there was something she did that may have triggered the negative attitude she was getting from him. Nothing seemed to come to mind. She wept most of the time and felt so alone in the marriage and didn't know how to solve this issue. It weighed her down and caused countless sleepless nights. She never imagined it was possible for one to be married, have a companion, and still feel all alone, but unfortunately that was her case with Donald. For her, the only difference between when she was single and now that she was married was that there was a man present in the house, since companionship was ultimately lacking.

She stayed awake most nights crying and in certain cases watching the stars outside of her window, as if she was expecting the stars to speak and let her know how to handle the matter or give her a sign to let her know that everything was going to be alright. She also felt that if Donald heard her cries in the silent night hours maybe he would be moved to change his behavior towards her, but that didn't seem to be the case, as he didn't even bother to ask why she was crying on such occasions. She finally decided not to bother him with such talks anymore, change her strategy towards the matter, and see if there could be any positive results.

One fateful day she approached him while he lay down and seemed to be in somewhat of a good mood and insisted that he accompany her to the mall for grocery shopping, with the intention of helping him understand how a couple needed to bond. Prior to making the request, she started off by making his favorite dish and after he was done eating, she asked him to accompany her to the mall to buy a few things for the house. As usual, her request was met with some resistance as he explained that he didn't feel like going to the mall.

Elly made up her mind that she was not taking no for an answer and insisted that he should accompany her to the mall. As she pestered him, Donald, realizing that she was not going to let the matter rest, reluctantly accepted, dressed, and drove to the mall, grumbling all the way there. When they arrived and paced around from one corner of the mall to another she tried to hold conversations with him, asking his view about certain things, cracking jokes, giggling and laughing as she spoke to see if he would lighten up. He was grumpy the entire time, making it clear that he didn't want to be there. All efforts at trying to have a conversation with her husband and enjoy their time together yielded no results, as it was obvious through his expressions and countenance that he wasn't happy. She became furious at his attitude and decided that was the last time she would make such requests of him.

Her home was no longer a place of fun, and she noticed that she was not excited to be there anymore, so she started spending more time in the office or doing volunteer work for some charities when she had less work in the office. On most occasions, she felt like she was sinking with no one to help, and she noticed this was also affecting her work output in the office.

Her performance at work started to deteriorate and the once shining star began to fade since she was emotionally unstable. This became noticeable to her colleagues and direct supervisor who called her aside one of the days to understand what was happening and why she was often moody. She explained that she had some personal family challenges but didn't really want to talk about the issue. Her boss, who understood that she wasn't ready to discuss the challenges she was facing, advised her to seek professional help. It was obvious to her colleagues that she was struggling. She thanked her for being understanding and for the words of admonition, stood up, went into the restroom, and wept for a while. She prayed silently and asked God to help her emotionally, and immediately her spirit was lifted, and she went back to work. After the conversation with her boss and realizing the extent to which the issues at home were affecting her work, she decided that henceforth she would try not to allow the issues she was facing to affect her work.

Elly continued to endure in silence as Donald continued to mistreat her, but she never failed to show him care and treat him with love, while he arrogantly told her on certain occasions that she couldn't do without him, pointing out that she loved him more than he loved her. If only he knew that every human being, both male and female has a breaking point, and she was getting to that point, maybe he might have acted differently.

She ultimately lacked every affection a woman required from her man, and wondered certain times if this was how marriage should be. As she thought about this, her mind shifted to her parents' marriage, and she remembered how affectionate her late father was towards her mother. She then realized that there was something lacking in her marriage, and she wept occasionally wondering why life was so unfair to her.

Donald continued this unfair treatment towards her for a little over two years, when Elly decided it was best to reach out to his family to seek assistance since she had a very good relationship with them at that point. She was gradually losing her mind, and she needed someone to help her.

It turned out that the decision to speak with his family didn't go down well with him since he always wanted to be regarded as the golden child of the family who wouldn't hurt a fly. Truly, his family had considered him the golden child because of his gentleness. They were surprised to hear that he was mistreating his wife that way. He felt hurt and was angry that Elly reported him and decided to punish her for what she did. He knew her weakness, which was that she disliked the silent treatment, as she was always restless whenever they were not on speaking terms, and he decided to prey on this weakness. "I will make her suffer immensely for what she has done," Donald thought to himself.

As expected, Elly became restless that Donald was ignoring her and she approached him repeatedly to ask for his forgiveness, explaining that she just needed to see if they could help her get through to him. "I never meant any harm, please pardon me," she pleaded with her husband. All pleas fell on deaf ears, as Donald refused to forgive her. She tried every method she could think of to get her husband to forgive her, but he hardened his heart. A few weeks later, he moved out of the bedroom which they shared, started sleeping in another room, and continuously kept his distance.

Elly cried day and night hoping that the tears would move him to forgive her, but he was reluctant and refused to speak to her and kept this attitude going for over six months. Suddenly, he started keeping late nights and she noticed that he seemed to have gotten involved with another woman. It was at this point that it became clear that this man who came to her as an angel of light, appearing calm and gentle, never loved or wanted her. He had told her on certain occasions that he loved her, only that he was not a romantic person, which is why it seemed like he wasn't giving her the attention she needed. However, she didn't believe this because she wondered how a man could treat a woman whom he claimed to love in such an ill manner and if he loved her, wouldn't her happiness be of utmost importance to him? She began to think back and remembered certain previous comments he made in the past which she didn't really take to heart at the time, but which now became clearer to her. "From all indications, I don't think his love for me was ever genuine," she muttered to herself.

As Elly pondered through all she had endured in the hands of Donald and circumstances surrounding her marriage and wondering if he ever loved her, she remembered the words of a prolific speaker and entertainment host, Steve Harvey, who once said that "All men can change and all men will change, but they only change for one woman, so if he isn't changing then that means you are not the woman." She thought about this statement for a while and wondered if Donald ever loved her even from the onset of the marriage. She expressed her frustrations to him regarding how she felt in the marriage, but he never listened or did anything to change it.

Since she didn't have any answers to all the questions running through her mind, she eventually decided to seek answers through prayers and earnestly prayed for peace of mind, which she eventually had despite all the issues she faced in the marriage. For a while, she struggled to understand how she ended up with a man who had nothing to offer her, including showing her any form of love and care. Who could she have possibly offended that such a terrible fate would come upon her?

13 | AN UNEXPECTED TURNAROUND

She lay on the floor to cry bitterly one day, and she heard a voice say, "If Sophia hadn't left her horrible marriage, how would she have known that her life could turn out this beautiful?" Sophia was a childhood friend who encountered similar issues in her first marriage. Sophia was so heartbroken when her ex-boyfriend whom she had dated for over four years left her to marry another woman. She became aware of the betrayal just a few days before the wedding and no reasonable explanation was provided by him for such callous treatment. She decided she was done with the whole dating concept and was going to marry the next available man, which turned out to be a big mistake. She kept to this decision and got married less than three months after being introduced to her first husband. Unfortunately, the marriage was short-lived as they separated one year into the marriage, citing irreconcilable differences. Well, that didn't come as a surprise to anyone since they barely knew each other prior to the wedding. During the separation period, she met her current husband who treated her so nicely and affectionately, and she got pregnant during their courtship, and gave birth to their first set of twin boys. They got married after the birth of the twins and had the second set of twins, this time around both girls. Life was more than sweet for Sophia, as her husband was very loving and tender towards her and they lived happily, with the family blossoming in every aspect. "Oh! How a woman blossoms once treated right by her man," which is a concept some men fail to understand. "A happy woman transcends to a happy and fruitful home." Now what if Sophia had decided to remain in the first marriage where this man treated her so horribly, "would she have experienced this sweet, wonderful home that she built with the man of her dreams?"

Immediately after she heard that voice and remembered Sophia's story, the tears seized, and she got up. She looked around to see if anyone was around that might have whispered that into her ears. Acknowledging that no one was there, and it was her subconscious, she got up from the floor, and wiped her tears. "I know what I must do to regain my peace and sanity. I must move on with my life since Donald is not ready for this marriage or ready to be a husband to me. After all, I'm not asking for much, but love, affection, and a little bit of attention from my husband" she said quietly to herself.

Elly assessed her present circumstance and wondered if there was any hope at all for herself and Donald. "Is there anything in this marriage worth fighting for or holding on to?" For her, there was absolutely nothing. She decided to move on and focus all her energy at work. She paid no more attention to the way she was treated in the marriage.

Donald, realizing that she was no longer feeling frustrated over his attitude towards her, or even paying him any attention, proceeded to walk away from her and the marriage. As she watched him walk away, she didn't feel sorry for herself or the situation anymore, rather it seemed like a huge burden was lifted. Her life suddenly became peaceful. All the questions she asked initially became clearer at that point. Donald never loved her. Why else would he walk away from her rather than find ways to fix the broken marriage, especially since he caused most of the issues.

She decided to pick up the broken pieces of her life and refused to let her present circumstances define her. After all, she was not the first person to be in such a situation, nor would she be the last. "A significant number of women endure even more distressing situations, yet they persevere," she murmured to herself. "Meanwhile, certain individuals silently suffer in fear of pursuing their best interests, possibly due to concerns about societal judgments. It perplexed her to think of the reasons why they placed such an intense focus on others' opinions, to the extent that it jeopardized their own lives. She had become acquainted with heart-wrenching stories, such as women remaining in abusive marriages until they were beaten to death. Given her experience and marital struggles, she decided it might be worthwhile to set up a practice firm to counsel intending couples and those struggling with marital issues with no one to guide them. But first she needed to equip herself either by reading the right books, partaking in certain professional courses, discussing with experts, and doing whatever might be necessary to gain the required skills.

14 | BUILDING A LASTING FOUNDATION

The skill acquisition process began, and she registered with a globally recognized institution focused on human psychology and counseling. Her goal was to set up a counseling and consultancy firm to help both intending and struggling couples, while incorporating learnings from her failed marriage to Donald.

At first her main reason for venturing into counseling was to help the girl child and protect them emotionally, since it was beginning to seem like society had failed them. On a second thought, she decided to make it broader, counseling both intending and married couples, since men also tend to experience marital abuses, with most refusing to speak up due to societal perceptions which expect men to be strong no matter what they face. This is wrong, because some men have battled severe depression in the past, and in severe cases have ended their lives rather than seeking help, due to this wrongful perception and expectation.

Men need to understand that it's okay to show emotions and feelings, and it doesn't make them less of a man. In fact, "a man who allows himself to be vulnerable and seek help when needed should be considered brave and there ought to be greater awareness of this."

Once she finalized her program and research and felt well, equipped for the task, she created awareness through the media, and with time she began receiving calls and bookings for her counseling sessions.

The counseling and consultancy firm kicked off fully, and she quit her job despite having a thriving career. She planned to focus solely on this new venture and ensure it succeeded.

Couples and singles sought her services from far and wide, and she helped most couples get back on track. For some people, her advice to them was to consider exploring other routes to achieving happiness given the complicated circumstances surrounding their relationships. As she counseled couples through their issues, she was astonished at the stories she encountered during the sessions and felt pity for most of them. She wondered how people could be so heartless to others, and wondered if they secretly gained any form of satisfaction causing others pain.

In her view, "a real man is known by how kind and loving he treats his woman, not how well he can play with different women's emotions, in the name of having fun and just being a man." Men need to understand that "women are structured in a way that enables them to magnify whatever they receive. If you give her love, she will return that to you in a hundred folds, but if you give her problems, she will double it and return it in hundred folds too." Except for a woman who is naturally difficult, she cannot be loved right by her man, and will not in turn give him peace of mind and a happy home.

Elly continued to counsel intending and married couples, and as time passed, she realized that most of the issues experienced by couples, especially the married ones, were centered around a lack of financial stability by the men. In various situations, she realized that it seemed most of these men took out their frustrations on their wives, who in most cases were trying their best to maintain a healthy home front, despite the financial challenges experienced. "People need to understand that these financial issues, just like other life challenges, are often temporary, and with hard work and passage of time they tend to go away." Once this concept is understood, it's easier for partners to work together to figure out the best way out.

She wondered if it was not advisable for a lady to marry a man who is not financially stable, because she realized that even when some of these women understood the man's present circumstances, are encouraging and helping him find ways to achieve a breakthrough, they still tend to make life unbearable for them as if the unfortunate circumstance was the woman's fault. "Don't they realize that these women are human beings with blood running through their veins and it's also not easy for them? Why can't they realize that not all women are materialistic, and some women just want happy homes?" As all these thoughts clouded her mind, she realized that asking women not to be with men who are financially unstable isn't the answer, because she also heard and saw cases where the woman turned out to be the bedrock of the man's financial increase or turn around. Most of these men are usually appreciative of the women who stood by them, respected and encouraged them through the challenging period of life. Also, there's a possibility that a man who is financially stable at a certain point in his life could suddenly lose everything due to circumstances beyond his control.

She decided that the key message to couples as it relates to finances was to help them understand how financial issues impact relationships and marriages if not well handled. This helps couples be better prepared in the event of occurrence. "Preparation and planning are useful keys to achieving success in anything, including a healthy and successful marriage." This issue of finances is a big elephant in the room, and couples need to be conscious of this fact, so they can decide how to address this in the event it occurs at any point of their relationship. "Understanding and planning is key to a successful marriage and relationship," she always advises.

She also advises intending couples to spend time understanding their partners, individual goals, family background and other key things worth knowing about each other before deciding if they wish to enter a marriage union. The wedding process is good and important, but the marriage itself is more important than just the wedding day. Elly never failed to state and explain that "the foundation of every marriage is essential and a key consideration for a happy and lasting union." Although every marriage is expected to have its peculiar issues and challenges at certain times given that it's a union of two individuals with different upbringings, the effect and impact on marriages with a proper foundation tend to be a bit reduced. For her, genuine love from both partners should be one of the key elements for any successful marriage, because if this exists between the couple, there's nothing they can't withstand together. Although love alone does not make a marriage successful, this must be one of the key pillars for couples to stand on and build upon.

An analogy of a proper foundation for relationships and marriages can be likened to the foundation of a house, which is the most important aspect of ensuring that a house withstands whatever is thrown at it as the building progresses into other stages. Now imagine that the house foundation is not right, there's a higher incidence of collapse when external forces and materials are added onto it, as it will not be able to withstand these pressures.

When she looked back at her experiences, she realized that her marriage to Donald would not have fallen apart if he genuinely loved her, because despite everything she did for him out of love, he never appreciated any and remained distant throughout the marriage. If Donald had loved her, he would have treated her better and wouldn't have the mind to completely ignore her for over six months due to a trivial issue they had when she reached out to his family to seek help regarding the issues they had. It's impossible that a man who loves his woman will ignore her for that extended period, especially when they lived in the same house, and he could see how much she was hurting from such treatment. "Love is kind and keeps no record of wrongdoing," so if a spouse can keep malice for that length of time over such a trivial issue, then it's okay to conclude that there's no love there, or maybe some people don't even understand the concept of love, since "you can't give what you don't have."

Another key area of concern she noted from counseling couples is the "aspect of female submission." While she didn't want to challenge people's views on submission given the controversies it tends to generate, one key message to men with such concerns is that "submission comes extremely easy for most women once they are treated right." Elly always gave them a task, without the knowledge of their wives, "to treat her like a queen, and make her feel like she was literally the only woman on earth and provide her feedback within three months on the wives' attitude." As it turned out, she frequently received positive feedback from some men, who finally understood the concept of submission. Just like stated earlier, "women tend to multiply whatever they are given, meaning that if you give her problems, she will return that back to you in multiple folds. Can you imagine giving her love and attention, she will treat you like the king of the castle." In a few cases, Elly didn't find it unusual that she received negative feedback from some men, because just like every other theory in life, there will be few exceptions, especially since some people can be very difficult to please. For her, it was a successful strategy given that most of the feedback received was positive.

She also explained to couples that although women are naturally expected to play a higher role in ensuring the success of their marriages, a successful marriage is based on a concerted effort between both parties. "Marriage can somewhat be likened to a business partnership, where each party must bring something to the table, goals aligned, and all parties responsible for its success." Individuals, both men and women, are also advised to know their limits when faced with a difficult spouse, especially one who continues to abuse them. "Don't let people make you feel that abuse is only physical, as it can come in different ways, both emotional and verbal. While physical abuse is physically manifested and people can see the marks, what of your mind, isn't that important too?" "Thankfully, there's a greater awareness of mental health," she said.

One main thing she learned from her experience with Donald and during the separation period was how people tend to be irrational, selfish, and often tend to hear what they want to hear. As such, she advises that "one needs to learn to put their foot down once they have decided on the right course of action, are at peace with whatever decision they are making, and should find ways to block out negativities and naysayers."

When her marriage to Donald ended, he continued spreading false narratives about what had occurred during their marriage. In an attempt to defend herself and make others understand the emotional trauma she had endured throughout their relationship, she noticed that most people were unwilling to listen or empathize. Instead, they held onto their own preconceived notions. She couldn't understand how people could judge her without even trying to understand the situation and what she endured in the marriage. She heard certain remarks such as "are you aware that some women are experiencing worse issues and have continued to endure?" And she responded with "what of those enjoying their marriages?" The constant comparison to those probably suffering in their marriages seemed to baffle her, as she wondered how people could be that shallow-minded. "Doesn't she deserve to be loved like others enjoying their marriages too?" She often asked them. Some women have been guilted into staying in abusive homes due to words like these, thereby leading to depression and untimely deaths in some cases. These same negative people will mourn briefly and move on with their lives, while some will still blame you for not leaving, showing that you can't please anyone. "So, isn't it better to just endure the negativities for a short while, stay alive, and be happy?"

For her, she knew that all those advising her and saying such negative things might probably act in worse ways if they had to endure all she did with Donald. She eventually noticed that most people who failed to understand the situation already had an expectation that because she was a woman, she was expected to find a way to make it work, even if the other party made no effort to fix the issue. She found it absurd that Donald didn't even for a day call to work things out, or even accept the mistakes he made. *"How do you fix a broken relationship when the other party deliberately refuses to come to terms with their actions, those that led to the current predicament?"* This is a recipe for disaster because it means that if you return to such a person, the same cycle of abuse will continue.

As she kept explaining and trying to get people to understand her, she realized that it seemed she was going around in circles and decided to stop explaining herself and simply moved on with her life. "Well, I can't be bothered to prove myself to anyone anymore or make them listen to me," Elly said to herself one day. For her, the peace of mind she had was important and she was grateful to God for giving her peace throughout the adversities she encountered. She was also comforted by the fact that her mother, close family, and a few friends understood her pains and stood by her through that challenging period of her life. Her decision to move on and stop explaining herself resulted from the realization that most people who chose not to understand her point of view were mainly from Donald's circle. She felt it was a bit understandable given that they either had a wrong motive for choosing not to understand or just like Elly, they had a wrong perception of him and were deceived by his calm demeanor. Few people who knew Donald often praised him for being so gentle and calm, but only Elly knew certain truths about him. I guess not only Elly judged a book by its cover. They seemed to be as naïve as she had been, when she first met him.

Based on her experiences and the peace she found after disregarding the negative things people said about the situation, she advises her clients to "develop strategies to block out negativities from people, and always remember to put yourself and emotions first when making certain important and life-changing decisions. Once you decide on the right course of action, make sure you are at peace with yourself and God, then forget whatever anyone has to say, because you alone wear the shoe and know where it pinches."

People should learn not to care so much about what society

has to say, because most people, particularly the women who have stayed in abusive homes, were always concerned about public perception, as they tend to care so much about what people would say if they left. In other cases, they have hinged it on the fact that they are staying because of their children, but they don't seem to understand the level of emotional damage they are inflicting on these children, particularly the male children, who tend to manifest these attributes when they are older. In most cases, they tend to repeat what they have learned from their parents' marriage, since they believe that is how their partners should be treated. "You can't sow thorns and expect to reap a bountiful harvest, couples need to be awake to this reality."

Growing up, Elly's mother had a close relation who complained about the maltreatment her daughter, Mayo received from her husband. The man repeatedly hit her even while she was pregnant, thereby leading to frequent miscarriages. When Mayo complained to her parents that she was being mistreated and beaten by her husband, they went to the house and picked her up. A few people intervened and after much pleading, the parents allowed her to return to the husband with a stern warning that if repeated, they would remove their daughter from the marriage permanently. The man who showed no remorse on how he was assaulting his wife made a remark in the presence of Mayo's mother saying, "Your daughter can leave as many times as she wishes but will always come back. If you don't believe me, go and ask my mother how many times she left her husband's house and still went back." The mother of this girl was astonished on hearing such words from the man, and when she made inquiries about the family, she learned of the incessant beatings the mother received from the father and she finally understood why he treated his wife in that manner. He grew up in an abusive environment, where his mother received frequent beatings and assumed that was how a man should treat a woman.

Mayo's parents eventually had to remove their daughter and grandson from the man's home since the beatings persisted just as they suspected. Also, they didn't want their grandson to learn these acts of domestic violence from his father.

Now, let's think about this logically, "what if the mother of this man was brave enough to take her children out of that abusive environment, wouldn't she have passed a vital message to her children, particularly the boys?" She would have taught them that "it's unacceptable to physically abuse a woman" and the boys will understand the implications of physically abusing their wives, which is that "they can walk away from them and the marriage if not treated right." This important lesson would have been inscribed in their minds from childhood.

The impact of family upbringing in marriages was obvious in certain cases Elly handled, as one could argue that part of the reason why some men were not good husbands to their wives resulted from circumstances surrounding their upbringing. It felt like they didn't understand what it meant to love a woman, since they never learned it from their fathers' who were supposed to be role models. This doesn't mean that it can't be fixed, however these affected individuals need to unlearn many things regarding relationships and marriage and be open to seeking counseling from trained professionals to get them back on track and renew their minds. This can only work if they are open to accepting their faults, and seeking the right guidance, after all no one can help a mature person who is not eager to help him/herself or does not see any fault in their actions.

Now, Elly's main goal for struggling couples was to help them develop tactics for obtaining different and better results. You can't expect to do something the same way and expect a different result. There needs to be a change in tactics and approach to achieve a different and possibly better result. However, if the individual believes he/she has tried everything possible and the only solution for peace of mind, which is very important, is to walk away, then that's what you must do, and pay no thought to whatever anyone has to say, she advises her clients.

When her marriage to Donald ended, she remembered how people said all manner of things about her, and made her feel sad and miserable at first, but eventually she developed a tough skin and didn't let any of their words affect her anymore. Within a short time, everyone had moved on to other things, and she was happy knowing that she was at peace and free from a man who had tortured her mostly emotionally. *"Be yourself and do you, the world will always adjust."*

15 | TWO HEARTS BEATING AS ONE

Her counseling and consultancy firm significantly expanded, enabling her to provide guidance to couples across numerous countries. As a result of her growing reputation, her expertise was sought after on multiple continents. In order to accommodate those unable to meet her in-person, she seamlessly conducted counseling sessions both in-person and online. She used various platforms to reach a large audience and educate them on key relationship concepts. She was invited to various seminars worldwide to speak on relationship matters, and she gained several recognitions and awards globally and became an international star.

Elly made a real impact in the lives of singles and couples, and helped couples understand that they had every right to demand better treatment from their partners and spouses or choose to walk away from abusive relationships. She made sure to emphasize that people shouldn't view physical abuse as the only form of domestic abuse, as it can come in various ways, including emotionally, financially, and/or verbally. Once it doesn't feel right, then it's definitely not right and everyone needs to be conscious of this fact and learn to protect their mental health at all costs.

She advises singles not to allow societal norms or any form of pressure to affect their choice of a partner, because it's better to remain single and find ways to be happy than be stuck in a loveless marriage. This is one of the surest ways to fall into depression if not handled and managed properly. Marriage is meant to be enjoyed, not endured.

During her seminars, she places a strong emphasis on the importance of pre-marital counseling. It's common for couples to think they have everything figured out, only to discover the reality of marriage is quite different. Going into marriage without premarital counseling is like a fresh graduate starting a new job without previous work experience or any training to prepare him/her for their role. Just as a graduate without experience would need technical training to acquire the basic skills required for their job, couples too should undergo pre-marital counseling to equip themselves and continue to learn and grow together, just like "on-the-job" training. Some companies who understand the importance of continuous training in improving job performance even go a step further by scheduling occasional training for their employees which is relevant to their respective roles. Elly remembered how she had to attend several training courses, including overseas training, when she worked with the international oil company, and how that better equipped and helped her to continuously improve her job performance. This is what counseling does for intending and married couples, she explained during the seminars, "as it equips them for the ride ahead with their partners."

Now let's imagine the fresh graduate is not trained and

equipped with the right skill, he/she will almost drown in the new role, except they seek assistance from an experienced person or get the right training.

She advised couples that missed on pre-marital counseling to seek post-marital counseling from professionals, and not take for granted the benefits of marital counseling in marriages. "It also does not mean having premarital counseling stops a couple from seeking occasional post-marital counseling, as both are necessary," she explained, and reminded them of the example she gave initially about the importance of regular training to ensure continuous improvement in job performance.

She remembered that with Donald, there was neither pre-marital nor post-marital counseling, hence, they were not equipped for the marriage. When she realized that things were falling apart, she had reached out to a counselor who agreed to meet with them for the post-marital counseling session. On presenting the idea to Donald, as usual, he was not interested in attending the session. He had told her that "there was nothing wrong with him, so he doesn't need the counseling session and she should go ahead to attend it alone." What baffled her most times with Donald was how he lived in denial throughout the marriage, even when it was clear that things were falling apart. He failed to accept that almost everything was going wrong with the marriage until it finally fell apart.

Elly looked back at her failed marriage to Donald. Remembering all she had to endure during the marriage and the negativities that surrounded her after the marriage ended, she realized that those experiences were shaping her for this present time in her life. Her experiences eventually turned out to be the stepping stone for the birthing of her inner potential. She could relate better during counseling sessions due to first-hand experience with some of these issues.

Turns out there was a silver lining at the end of the tunnel. "When you go through tough times in life, remember it's only for a moment in time and it will surely pass," she advises. Never lose hope and faith.

On the last day of one of the seminars she had abroad which recorded a huge attendance of guests, she was walking out of the hall when her eyes suddenly caught a familiar face and she paused, She walked over to confirm the person she just saw. As she got closer, she noticed it was an old friend from the university, as suspected, and it was Richard's closest friend. They exchanged pleasantries and he introduced Elly to his wife who sat beside him. Since she was about to leave and a few people were waiting to see her, they exchanged contacts and agreed to catch up in a few days, since they hadn't seen each other in a long time.

Two days afterwards, they met in one of the restaurants, and caught up on events in the past years. She asked him about Richard, and he confirmed they were still in contact. She requested Richard's contact, since the last time they spoke was about four years ago on her wedding night. He called out of the blue, and she had explained to him that it was the night of her wedding. He congratulated her, and never called back, probably because he felt she was gone forever, being married to someone else.

Elly never thought about the experience until that moment when she spoke with Richard's friend. She suddenly became curious, wondering why he called her on that day, especially since they hadn't spoken for over five years prior to that very day.

He gave her Richard's number and explained that he lived in the same country where she was for the seminar. Elly decided she was going to call him just to know what prompted him to call her on that fateful wedding night. She also wanted to catch up with him after many years apart. They chatted for a few more minutes, bid each other farewell, and she went back to her hotel room.

The next morning, she called Richard's number about three times, but there was no response and she decided to give it a rest for another hour before she called again. She called back and this time, a female voice answered, and since she could barely understand what the person was saying, she felt that maybe the number was incorrect and decided not to bother anymore. A few minutes later, she received a call from the same number and this time it was a male's voice, but not Richard's. She always recognized his voice, and it didn't sound like him. She proceeded to ask if it was Richard on the phone and the person replied, "Yes." Although it didn't sound like him, she continued speaking and then suddenly felt a switch to the voice she remembered and could feel the excitement in his voice as they spoke. They spoke for a while and since the conversation grew longer, Elly explained that she was around for a seminar and would be leaving the country in a few days. They agreed to meet up the next day.

The day approached, and she was a bit nervous, since they hadn't seen each other in over ten years, and she didn't know what to expect. However, as they saw each other on that day, there seemed to be so much love in their eyes, and it felt as if their hearts connected again and the spark which existed between them was rekindled. This wasn't what she was expecting was going to happen when she called, because all she was trying to find out was why he called that night, and here she is gazing into his eyes, and there was so much love in them.

For some minutes, they were both lost for words, and kept staring into each other's eyes before Richard finally broke the silence and asked how she was doing. Prior to their meeting, Richard heard about her fame just like most people, but he hadn't bothered to reach out, because the last time they spoke she had just got married, so he moved on believing he had lost her forever.

Elly explained the situation with her previous marriage and gave a summary of her life history since they broke up and asked about Richard's situation since she was aware that he also had gotten married—even before her. He explained that his previous marriage also crashed many years ago, and he hadn't remarried since then, and the lady that picked up his phone earlier was his girlfriend who came over to visit. He explained that he was certain that the lady was going to be his ex-girlfriend soon, because she stormed out of the house after seeing the excitement on his face when Elly called. She realized it was his first love that he told her about when they first met.

Richard never failed to mention Elly to the people that were important in his life, so most people around him knew about her even though they separated many years ago. He never got over Elly even after the relationship ended, including after getting married to his ex-wife. She was his one true love, and nobody could ever take her place in his heart, even after being apart for years and meeting several women. Elly was surprised to hear all that, and it was at this point she realized that since her relationship with Richard ended, she never met any man that shared the type of love they once had. She wondered if this was really her true love.

She thought about her relationship journey over the years, including the heartbreaks she suffered, and remembered how Richard told her when she broke up with him, that "no man will love her the way he did." He knew from the onset that Elly was his soul mate.

As she gazed into the open space, and listened to Richard speak, tears flowed down her eyes, as she wished she had listened to him then and forgiven him for that mistake. Maybe she might not have experienced the heartaches she felt from those men in the past. Richard hugged and consoled her as she cried, promising that he was never going to leave her side again or cause her to ever shed any tears in the future if she gave him another chance. As she dried her tears, she asked him why he called her on that wedding night, because she had thought about it lately, and felt it was a bit unusual that he would call her on that fateful day, given they hadn't spoken for years. She asked if he heard about the wedding and decided to call, or why exactly he decided to call on that day. He explained that no one had told him about the wedding, and since they had been separated for a very long time, they didn't have any mutual friends that would inform him about the wedding. He explained that on his way home from work that evening, he felt moved in his spirit to call her, and he initially shoved the feeling away since they hadn't spoken in a very long time, but as he continued to feel restless, he dialed her number on his phone, and that was when he realized that she was married that day.

Elly was surprised at his explanation and was amazed how much they connected to each other, that he could be moved in his spirit that way, almost as if something was telling him that a part of him was being taken away by another man. It was at this point that she realized how many years they had wasted being apart from each other, since it was clear their hearts beat for each other, and not even passage of time could stop them from loving each other. Since their relationship ended, she had never felt this type of connection with any other man, and Richard also felt the same way. Here they were in each other's presence and all the love they once shared came rushing back, and it seemed as if it was even stronger than before.

Richard explained to Elly to give him just a few days to sort out his life with the number of ladies he was seeing, since at that point his lifestyle was not the best. He promised to sever all ties with them, with the aim of focusing solely on her. He wasn't going to make the same mistake that led to the relationship with the love of his life ending. He was going to be fully committed this time and love her until his dying breath. This action taken by Richard confirmed what Elly always knew and taught her clients, which is that when a man truly loves a woman, the love he has for her causes him to change or act right, and you don't need to persuade or force any man to change.

Elly traveled back home. They began dating again, and became inseparable, as they spoke for hours every day. A few weeks later, he introduced her to his family members who already knew her from the first time they dated, since he always made sure that his friends and family knew how much she meant to him. Richard always knew from the onset that she was his wife. He wasn't going to take any chances with losing her to any man this time, so he traveled down to the country where she was based just a few months after they reunited and proposed to her.

Although Elly always told herself that she was going to spend time dating and fully get to know the next man that asks for her hand in marriage, she couldn't turn him down, because from every indication it was clear that this was her true love and it felt so right when he proposed. She however prayed about the decision and asked God that "if this isn't the right man for me, let the relationship come to a natural end," since she wasn't ready to have another failed marriage. The relationship continued to blossom and got stronger with every passing day, and she felt convinced in her heart that this was her "prince charming."

They agreed and fixed a date for their wedding ceremony which was attended by just a few friends and close family members since they agreed that they didn't want many guests at the ceremony.

Richard loved Elly so much and made her feel so loved through both his words and actions. Elly was so happy and grateful that she found a love so genuine and pure in him, and she thanked God daily for blessing her with such a wonderful, loving, and caring husband.

She realized that everything she lacked and complained about in her previous marriage was done effortlessly by Richard, which proved what she had always known, that when a man truly loves a woman, you don't beg for his attention, as he wants to do anything within his means to see his woman happy.

The marriage was fruitful and blessed with two children, a boy and girl, just as Elly had always desired, and they lived happily ever after in their country home.

ABOUT THE AUTHOR

Chikaodi E. Chinwuba is the author behind *A Promise of Dawn*, a captivating and inspiring work of fiction. This wonderful novel not only takes readers on an adventure, but also provides valuable guidance for navigating life's challenges, particularly in the realm of relationships.

Chikaodi honed her writing skills through her experiences in financial consulting. She has collaborated with prestigious international accounting firms, assisting numerous high-value clients in gaining a deep understanding of their transactions.

In addition to her successful career, Chikaodi is happily married to her soulmate, whom she met during her university years. Their bond remains strong and continues to flourish.